"Holly...Holly...can you possibly know what you do to me?"

Jake whispered.

I know what you do to *me,* she thought. You cut me loose from every mooring of sanity and prudence.

Aloud she said, "What just happened now was as much my fault as yours. But it can't be repeated...I have a ten-year-old stepdaughter to think about."

Astonished, Jake didn't answer.

She persisted, "I want your word that, in the future, you'll keep your hands to yourself."

Tight-lipped and still hot with desire, Jake regarded her with narrowed eyes. If she kicked me off the ranch, it would serve me right, he acknowledged—not for kissing her, but for the deception I'm practicing.

Dear Reader,

Enjoy the bliss of this holiday season as six pairs of Silhouette Romance heroes and heroines discover the greatest miracle of all…true love.

Suzanne Carey warms our hearts once again with another **Fabulous Father**: *Father by Marriage*. Holly Yarborough thought her world was complete with a sweet stepdaughter until Jake McKenzie brightened their lives. But Jake was hiding something, and until Holly could convince him to trust in her love, her hope of a family with him would remain a dream.

The season comes alive in *The Merry Matchmakers* by Helen R. Myers. All Read Archer's children wanted for Christmas was a new mother. But Read didn't expect them to pick Marina Davidov, the woman who had broken his heart. Could Read give their love a second chance?

Moyra Tarling spins a tale of love renewed in *It Must Have Been the Mistletoe*. Long ago, Mitch Tyson turned Abby Roberts's world upside down. Now he was back—but could Abby risk a broken heart again and tell him the truth about her little boy?

Kate Thomas's latest work abounds with holiday cheer in *Jingle Bell Bride*. Sassy waitress Annie Patterson seemed the perfect stand-in for Matt Walker's sweet little girl. But Matt found his temporary wife's other charms even more beguiling!

And two fathers receive the greatest gift of all when they are reunited with the sons they never knew in Sally Carleen's *Cody's Christmas Wish* and *The Cowboy and the Christmas Tree* by DeAnna Talcott.

Happy Reading!

Anne Canadeo
Senior Editor

Please address questions and book requests to:
Silhouette Reader Service
U.S.: 3010 Walden Ave., P.O. Box 1325, Buffalo, NY 14269
Canadian: P.O. Box 609, Fort Erie, Ont. L2A 5X3

FATHER BY MARRIAGE

Suzanne Carey

Silhouette
R O M A N C E™
Published by Silhouette Books
America's Publisher of Contemporary Romance

Special thanks to Mr. Amos Cordova of the Durango & Silverton
Railroad, Durango, Colorado, for his help with my research.
Though my heroine in *Father by Marriage* was too distraught to
appreciate it to the fullest, the ride on a coal-powered train from
Durango to Silverton, high in the southern Rockies, has to be one
of the most spectacular and thrilling a person can take!

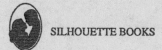 SILHOUETTE BOOKS

ISBN 0-373-19120-0

FATHER BY MARRIAGE

Copyright © 1995 by Verna Carey

Books by Suzanne Carey

Silhouette Romance

A Most Convenient Marriage #633
Run, Isabella #682
Virgin Territory #736
The Baby Contract #777
Home for Thanksgiving #825
Navajo Wedding #855
Baby Swap #880
Dad Galahad #928
Marry Me Again #1001
The Male Animal #1025
The Daddy Project #1072
Father by Marriage #1120

Silhouette Intimate Moments

Never Say Goodbye #330
Strangers When We Meet #392
True to the Fire #435
Eleanora's Ghost #518

Silhouette Desire

Kiss and Tell #4
Passion's Portrait #69
Mountain Memory #92
Leave Me Never #126
Counterparts #176
Angel in His Arms #206
Confess to Apollo #268
Love Medicine #310
Any Pirate in a Storm #368

Silhouette Books

Silhouette Summer Sizzlers 1993
"Steam Bath"

SUZANNE CAREY

is a former reporter and magazine editor who prefers to write romance novels because they add to the sum total of love in the world.

Jake McKenzie on Fatherhood...

It's a funny thing, Lisa. I always wanted a daughter. But when you were "born" to me, during the Christmas Eve wedding ceremony in which I married Holly, your stepmother, you were already ten years old.

I'll never forget the first time I saw you. Getting off the school bus with your book bag and your artwork and your mop of red hair flying, you ran up the driveway like a young colt, frisky and bent on living life to the fullest. Besotted as I already was with Holly after knowing her just a couple of hours, I paused and thought somewhere deep inside myself, "Now, there's a kid I could love."

You say I've taught you stuff. Well, you've taught me so much. One of the most important things is that people in a family don't have to be related to each other. All they need is love. If Holly and I are lucky enough to make you a baby sister someday, you and she will be like two peas in a pod in my heart.

I love you, Lisa.

Jake

Chapter One

"**I** want you to find her...*whatever it takes.*"

Seated behind the massive, carved-oak desk that dominated his study at the famed Flying D Ranch, Colorado real-estate-and-mining magnate Wiley E. "Dutch" Hargrett drove home the demand with a blunt stab of his cigar. His craggy salt-and-pepper eyebrows bristled, giving the words added emphasis. Accustomed to twinkling affably unless there was serious business to discuss, his myopic gray eyes burned with fierce determination behind his spectacles.

It was to be a command performance, then.

His back to the sweep of mullioned windows that overlooked the multimillion-dollar spread's magnificent stands of aspen and ponderosa pine, tough, high-powered lawyer Jake McKenzie didn't answer for a moment. Tall, rangy, dark-haired, good-looking in a rugged, outdoor sense that clashed subtly with his expensive pin-striped suit, he exuded a restless, faintly disillusioned air, as if the life he'd made for himself with grit, intelligence and sheer hard work had failed to satisfy.

At the moment, his priorities included discussing several pending legal matters with Dutch and the lengthy vacation he was determined to take just as soon as he could clear his calendar. The very last thing he wanted was to mount a personal search for Dutch's granddaughter, Lisa, whom a private detective had been unable to locate.

Mildly, because Dutch was a personal friend in addition to being his firm's most important client, Jake responded that the firm of Fordyce, Lane and McKenzie wasn't in the business of locating missing persons. He and his partners weren't trained investigators. They left that sort of thing to the experts.

"Maybe another detective..." he suggested.

With the single-mindedness that had helped make him a millionaire several times over, Dutch shook his head. "I want you," he insisted.

Lisa was the result of a brief affair between Dutch's and his wife Bernie's only child, thirty-four-year-old Dawn Hargrett, who was currently serving prison time in North Dakota for cocaine dealing, and the late Clint Yarborough, who'd been fatally injured when a rodeo stunt he'd attempted had gone awry, and she was all the Hargretts had. Yet she might be living in squalor somewhere. They wanted her *home*, in Durango, with them.

"She was last seen in the company of her stepmother, Yarborough's widow, shortly after his death," Dutch continued, naming the small Texas town where Clint Yarborough's rodeo accident had taken place. "A couple of years earlier, Yarborough hit it lucky. He won a minor lottery prize of several hundred thousand dollars. Supposedly, he bought a modest ranch with his winnings...somewhere in northern New Mexico or southern Colorado. I guess he sank most of the money in it, or ran through his reserves pretty quick, because he went back to the rodeo circuit a couple of years later, and got himself gored by a bull. Dollars to doughnuts the widow and Lisa returned to the ranch, at least long enough to put it on the market. If you can find it, you can probably pick up their trail."

Jake frowned. Having grown up poor on a small, down-at-the-heels ranch in southern Idaho and done some rodeo work himself to supplement his GI-bill-subsidized college and law-school tuition, he could sympathize with the financial difficulties Clint Yarborough had faced. As it happened, he'd met Clint once, at some fairgrounds or other, and rather liked the tall, taciturn cowboy with a face full of freckles and thinning, reddish hair.

Years later, after he and his increasingly successful law firm had landed Dutch as a client, he'd met Dawn Hargrett, as well. A spoiled, pouty Madonna-type used to getting her way with men, she'd propositioned him, then tried to get him in hot water with her father when he wouldn't cooperate.

She's a piece of work, all right, Jake thought with a wry purse of his lips—trouble if she so much as looks in a man's direction. In light of Clint's affair with Dawn, with whom he'd apparently cohabited less than a month, he wondered what kind of woman the lanky cowboy had seen fit to marry. One with scruples and maternal instincts, I'll bet, he thought, if she hasn't delivered Lisa to the Hargretts and demanded a hefty finder's fee.

There weren't that many loving, principled women running around loose in the world, in Jake's opinion. In his heart of hearts, he suspected their scarcity was one of the reasons for his disillusionment.

"I don't see how I could go after your granddaughter, even if I wanted to, with the Blackwell project on the table," he objected.

Dutch dismissed the importance of the hostile takeover his mining conglomerate was trying to engineer with a negligent wave of his hand. "Brent Fordyce can handle it with a little advice from you," he answered. "Nothing much is going to happen for the next couple of months, anyway." He paused. "I'd offer you a bonus if I thought you'd accept."

Though he was scarcely in Dutch Hargrett's league when it came to material wealth, these days Jake had all the money he needed. On the other hand, his premier client's reference to a "couple of months" dangled in front of his inner man like a plum just out of reach. Lately, he'd been feeling burned out, fidgety...soul hungry. He needed a rest. More than that, a change of scene. Sufficient time to regroup, search for new meaning in life, get reacquainted with the kind of fresh air and mountain scenery that had been a hallmark of his youth.

Abruptly, he found himself abandoning the idea of a traditional vacation in favor of a genuine leave of absence from the firm. Rethinking his refusal to hunt for the older man's granddaughter, he regarded Dutch with a thoughtful air. "To tell you the truth, I could use a breather," he admitted. "Of course, you realize that if I took several months' sabbatical and agreed to search for Lisa during my absence, I wouldn't be available here in Durango, at your beck and call."

His wish knocking on the door of fulfillment, Dutch was all ears. "Then you'll do it!" he exclaimed.

Jake had no intention of being bulldozed. "Hold on," he cautioned. "If I agree to go, my partners must be willing to take up the slack. *You'll* have to give me plenty of leeway.

Refrain from leaning on me for instant results. The search will be part investigation, part respite from my regular routine and I plan to take my time with it. I won't be checking in with you every day. Or even every week. Still, I don't see why finding the girl should prove that difficult...."

What might have been a tear of renewed hope slid down one of Dutch's leathery cheeks and was quickly brushed aside. "My boy, I don't know how to thank you," he whispered.

Jake pretended not to notice the breach in Dutch's tough-guy demeanor. "There's no need to thank me until I locate her," he said. "Are you sure the detective you hired checked official property records in the counties where you believe Clint Yarborough may have bought his spread?"

Dutch shrugged. "He claims he did—that he couldn't find a trace."

The prospect of succeeding where the detective had failed was pleasing to Jake. "I gather I've got your word, then," he reiterated. "No nagging. No pressure. I can take all the time I need . . . and want."

"Yes to all of the above."

Getting to their feet, the two men shook on it, with equally firm handgrips.

"Naturally, I hope you won't take too long," Dutch added, reclaiming an inch or so of the territory he'd relinquished. "We haven't laid eyes on Lisa since shortly before Dawn's arrest. She was going on five then. Bernie and I want a chance to know her and love her before she's all grown up."

Jake's request that his law partners, Brent Fordyce and Harry Lane, fill in for him while he was on leave met with little resistance once he'd informed them he'd be doing the firm's most prestigious client a personal favor. The following afternoon, having cleared his desk and read the lackluster detective's report Dutch had handed him, he was packing for his trip.

For once, instead of stashing custom-made shirts, designer suits and silk ties in a supple leather garment bag, he was tossing jeans and flannel shirts into a beat-up canvas valise. Scuffed and curling up at the toes from several decades of wear, his oldest pair of cowboy boots awaited him.

As he removed his gold Tissot timepiece from his wrist and placed it in his bedroom safe for the duration, he smiled at the callused condition of his palms. Thanks to the work he'd done himself, finishing off the new log home and barn he'd built on a prime twenty-seven-acre parcel just outside Durango, his hands wouldn't give him away. Neither would the secondhand truck he'd been using to haul lumber and other building materials to the site. Or the watch with a cracked crystal and worn leather strap that had seen him through his tour of duty as an eighteen-year-old medic's assistant near the end of the Vietnam War.

In addition to being comfortable and well suited to his mood, his old, unpretentious duds would provide excellent cover for his purposes. People weren't always comfortable talking to lawyers or prosperous-looking strangers. If and when they met, he knew Holly Yarborough wouldn't be. Dressed like the dirt-poor cowpoke he'd once been, he could spin her a line about being an old friend of Clint's, down on his luck. Or pretend he was an odd-jobs drifter, looking for work, close to needing a handout. She wouldn't recognize him as the well-heeled enemy.

For some reason, though he knew next to nothing about Clint Yarborough's widow beyond the fact that she was thirty-four years old, a former first-grade teacher who'd married the father of one of her pupils and taken up ranching with him, he was intrigued by the prospect of meeting

her. In part, he supposed, that was because of the anticipated thrill of the chase, in which he viewed Lisa as the prize
and Holly Yarborough as his adversary. Yet the theory
didn't totally explain what he felt.

Ironically, because they were on opposite sides of the
fence, the *idea* of her appealed to him. Pledged to further
Dutch's cause as both friend and attorney, he found her
decision to raise the Hargretts' granddaughter by herself
after her husband's death and steer clear of any entangle-
ment with them somehow exemplary.

If she was deliberately keeping Lisa from Bernie and
Dutch, as they suspected, it wasn't too difficult to guess her
reasons. Dawn would be eligible for parole in just eight
months. If she was released, the Hargretts would be all too
likely to reunite her and Lisa if they could. Idolizing Dawn
and blinding themselves to her faults, they might go so far
as to place Lisa in her care. And that would be a disaster, in
Jake's opinion.

Though his sense of fairness dictated that every ex-convict
should be given a second chance, and he agreed wholeheartedly that the Hargretts deserved contact with their
grandchild, instinct told Jake he and the unknown Holly
were in accord about the dangers of Dawn's influence.
Why'd you agree to search for Lisa, if that's how you feel?
he asked himself ironically, retrieving his padded and
hooded winter parka from the back of his closet in case cold
weather set in before he returned. Have your ethics become
that profit motivated?

He certainly hoped that wasn't the case. Relaxing a little
into the beginning of his leave, he decided to take a wait-
and-see attitude. Before reporting back to Dutch or setting
a custody suit in motion against her, he'd check Holly Yarborough out as thoroughly as he could—attempt to see the
issues of her stepdaughter's welfare the way she saw them.

*   *   *

Two and a half weeks later, at Honeycomb Ranch in a mountain-fringed valley near the small, somewhat isolated town of Larisson, Colorado, Holly Yarborough was cutting the wire fastenings from a bale of new shingles intended for the barn roof as she mentally grappled with a problem that seemed all but insurmountable. The previous afternoon, her hired man had quit, leaving her and Lisa to run the ranch alone.

During the past four years, two of them under Clint's tutelage and two on her own, she'd learned a lot about ranching. And that was just the trouble. She knew from experience that there were things a woman and a ten-year-old girl couldn't accomplish without help. *I'll have to find a replacement if I'm to keep Honeycomb operating so Lisa can inherit it someday,* she thought, grimacing with effort as the wire cutter in her gloved hand bit into the stubborn bindings.

Unfortunately for them, Clint's modest lottery winnings had long since vanished, and profits from the herd they'd been trying to expand into a sizable holding had been skimpy, at best. As a result, she couldn't afford to pay prospective help the going rate. To make matters worse, there wasn't anyone to whom she could turn for financial help. Both her parents had been dead for years. Her nearest living relatives were second cousins who lived on the east coast.

I'll die before I ask the Hargretts to bail us out, she vowed as the wire binding gave way, whipping across her denim-clad thigh. In fact, she wasn't even tempted. Since quitting her teaching career to marry Clint and settle on a cattle ranch with him, she'd loved his redheaded, freckle-faced daughter as her own. The two of them were very close.

There's nothing I wouldn't do for Lisa, she thought, straightening and pushing a stray wisp of blond hair out of her eyes. *No sacrifice would be too great.*

Clint's dying plea had only strengthened her resolve. As he lay gored by a bull in the back of the ambulance that was rushing him to the hospital, the man she'd married had begged her to keep his daughter away from her maternal grandparents.

"They'll take her from you . . . give her to Dawn," he'd warned, coughing up blood in his effort to speak. "And Dawn will ruin her. By the time she's fifteen, she'll be foul-mouthed . . . pregnant . . . on drugs. Thank God we put the ranch in your maiden name, so they won't be able to find you. Promise me, Holly . . . you'll raise her without their input."

Unknown to Holly as Clint's words echoed in her head, Jake was passing through Larisson, bringing involvement with the Hargretts straight to her door. Though he'd struck out in Texas, where no one seemed to have known Clint very well, or remember his wife and child, he'd done better in Taos, New Mexico. It was in Taos that Clint's now-deceased great-aunt had cared for Lisa while he'd traveled from one rodeo and dusty county fair to another, a single dad desperately trying to earn a living for them—there that Holly had taught school, making friends with her fellow teachers, who continued to nurture a warm regard for her. By asking around, Jake had learned Holly's maiden name and the fact that she'd married Clint in Chimayo, on the high road to Santa Fe.

Though nobody had been able to produce her current address, several people had tentatively pointed him toward Colorado and their information had been good. Earlier that afternoon, immersed in property deeds at the Bonino County courthouse, he'd turned up the name of one Holly Neeson and located the plat book that set forth the coordinates of her ranch. Incredibly, she and Lisa had been under

their noses all along—less than sixty miles from the Flying
D and his Durango law offices!

Content though Jake was with his own investigative
prowess, which had left the detective Dutch had hired in the
shade, he almost regretted running her to ground so easily.
Still, he was whistling as he drove, more invigorated than
he'd been in months. It would be tough to feel anything but
fantastic on a day like today, he admitted, with the mission
he'd undertaken verging on success, the early October sun
dazzling the meadows and great drifts of aspen shimmering
like yellow fire on the mountainsides. Yet he knew the lion's
share of his excitement flowed from none of those things. In
large measure, it derived from the unknown quantity of
Holly Yarborough herself, whom chance and Dutch Hargrett's stubbornness had placed directly in his path.

Since leaving Durango and spending more nights than not
in his sleeping bag under the stars, Jake had transformed her
into a legend in his imagination. The odds that she'd measure up caused his grin to broaden as he considered them. In
the flesh, he realized, the woman who'd frustrated Dutch's
efforts to find her could turn out to be ugly, mean spirited
or both—a clone of the evil stepmothers found in so many
fairy tales. At best, she was probably the feminine equiva-
lent of commercially baked bread, bland and doughy in its
mass-produced wrappers.

Grinning at his own perverse sense of humor, Jake
glanced at the directions he'd jotted down and turned from
the hard-surface highway he'd been following onto a dusty
secondary road with a gravel surface. As usual, the truth
probably lay somewhere in between. If he was a betting
man, he'd wager the woman he sought would turn out to be
as nice as her Taos friends thought, but no goddess in blue
jeans. When they finally met, he'd be forced to consign the
paragon he'd created to fill his need for romance and a

woman who'd restore his faith in her gender to the scrap heap.

The shingles freed of their wire bindings, Holly hauled out the extension ladder and propped it against the wall of the barn nearest the second-story entrance to the hayloft. She supposed she ought to check out the plywood subroofing before fastening on Clint's carpenter's apron and dragging a bunch of shingles to one of the upper rungs. According to her former hired man, who'd ripped off the damaged shingles in the area that needed patching before going on a three-day drunk and quitting her cold, a sizable portion of it needed to replaced.

About to clamber up for a look, she noticed a cloud of gravel dust mushrooming in the distance. Somebody was headed her way—probably the mailman. Though her mail usually consisted of a stack of bills she found difficult to pay, she decided to hike the quarter mile that separated her house and barn from the county-maintained highway and pick it up before continuing with her task.

To her surprise, the flag on her box was down. Her mail carrier had already deposited today's quota.

A couple of minutes later, Jake rounded a bend in the road that brought her ranch into view. To his astonishment, *there she was,* Lisa Yarborough's stepmother and the woman of his quixotic daydreams, a slim but shapely Scandinavian blonde whose sun-streaked hair was plaited in a single braid that fell between her shoulder blades. Busy removing mail from her country mailbox, she glanced up at his approach.

Boy, were you ever wrong, Jake thought, appreciatively noting the rounded but slender curves that filled out her faded, five-pocket jeans and plaid flannel shirt as he stopped his dusty, beat-up truck a few feet from her. She's a far cry from witch look-alikes. Or store-bought bread. Your notion of a goddess in blue jeans wasn't so preposterous.

Her mail held in one tentative, ungloved hand, Holly Yarborough gazed at him with a puzzled frown, as if she were attempting to make out his identity.

"Excuse me, ma'am," he said, getting out of the truck. "I'm just passing through…looking for some kind of work. Would you happen to know of anyone around here who has a job open? Or some odd chores that need doing? Right now, I'd settle for food…a little gas money. Maybe a place to spend the night."

Continuing to clutch her mail, which included another late notice from her mortgage company, Holly studied him. Rangy, big shouldered, with a narrow waist, muscular build and several stubby days' growth of beard, the stranger who had stopped at her gate in search of employment appeared to be down on his luck. His words only confirmed that impression. Yet something in his eyes, which were narrowed against the strong sunlight, begged to differ. For a drifter, he seemed to have a strong sense of himself.

After the long neutrality of her marriage to Clint and a two-year widowhood, she was undone by her strong reaction to him. Everything about him interested her. With a sudden, keen appreciation for detail, she found herself visually tracing the laugh lines that bracketed his mouth, and wondering how that mouth would feel pressed against hers. Sex appeal radiated from every inch of him.

A greater threat to her composure lay in his eyes. Sky mirrors of unadulterated blue, they seemed to gaze into her soul as if he expected to seek his fortune there. Yet she didn't harbor the slightest doubt that they'd registered every aspect of her physical self.

The sudden, gut-level tug was a new experience for her. From the beginning with Clint, her emotions had been gentle and sweet, not unruly and passionate. She'd never been swept off her feet by anyone.

How pretty and wholesome she looks, Jake thought, his jaded sensibilities quickening. More than he could say, he liked the long, pale lashes that shaded her eyes, the soft way her lips parted as she gazed up at him. With their short, clean-scrubbed nails, her hands were slim and capable looking. Her cheeks were lightly flushed, as if he'd unnerved her out of proportion to his question.

For her part, Holly needed a hired hand. This dark-haired stranger looked able. He didn't strike her as a potential thief or rapist. Yet she knew having him at Honeycomb for any length of time would be awkward if he kept undressing her with his eyes. Maybe it would be all right to let him stay for a day or two, she reasoned. He could help me get a leg up on mending the barn roof and replacing some of the fencing.

"Actually, I have a few things that need doing around here," she volunteered after a lengthy pause. "Mainly fencing, carpentry stuff. My hired man...is away just now. You could sleep in his trailer...stay a couple of days if you want. I'm a pretty good cook. Interested?"

The offer was tailor-made. If he accepted, Jake would be able to check her out—learn firsthand what kind of mother she was. He still wasn't sure what he would do with the information. As Dutch's attorney, he had a duty to serve the strong-willed older man's best interests. Yet he supposed a case could be made for them being synonymous with his granddaughter's. If things worked out the way he suddenly hoped they might, maybe he could serve as a go-between, effect a compromise of some sort.

Besides, he thought with a wry twist of humor that only glinted in his eyes, you'd be crazy to let a woman like Holly Yarborough slip through your fingers. To his appreciative eyes, she looked like a potential cure for what ailed him.

"That sounds good to me," he said, stifling any lingering scruples as he held out his hand. "This valley's a mighty pretty place. I'm Jake McKenzie—born and raised on a ranch in Idaho. I can start right now, if you want."

He hadn't said where he hailed from now. Or asked if there was a man about the place. She gathered he knew there wasn't. At least the calluses she noted testified he was no stranger to physical labor. "Okay, then," she answered, tentatively shaking hands with him and doing her best to quell the little shiver of excitement she felt. "I'm Holly Yarborough. I live here with my daughter, Lisa. If you'll give me a ride up to the barn, I'll show you where to park your truck."

"Great." He held the passenger door open for her.

A quick glance around the cab's interior as he took his place behind the wheel didn't tell her much—just that he didn't smoke or litter his surroundings with junk-food wrappers. Aside from a ballpoint pen, crumpled scrap of paper, cheap sunglasses and the beat-up valise he'd stashed behind the seat, it was devoid of personal effects.

During their brief ride up the dusty, quarter-mile track that separated her mailbox from the barn, Holly was glad his vehicle had a floor-mounted gearshift. Though his hand hovered close to her knee as he reached for it, the gear formed a kind of barrier between them.

She couldn't help noticing the long, lean thigh muscle that rippled beneath faded denim as he adjusted his pressure on the gas pedal. Or responding to the pheromone assault his proximity was mounting on her senses. She'd have to harden her heart before it got out of hand. Falling for a drifter—even a personable, good-looking one—was totally out of the question.

Like the place Jake had built himself on twenty-seven rolling acres outside Durango, Holly Yarborough's ranch house was constructed of logs and situated near a creek. But there the similarity ended. Smaller and older, it had mortared seams, a steeply pitched roof that would allow snow to slide off easily in winter and a rough fieldstone chimney. An old-fashioned veranda ran the width of the simple, octagonal structure. On it, someone had placed a pair of split-ash rockers. There were crisp, white curtains at all the windows.

"The trailer's on the other side of the barn," she advised, getting out of the truck as he braked by the corral. "You can park there. I've got some iced tea in the fridge. Would you like some before we get to work?"

Jake nodded. The dusty roads had made him thirsty.

"I was about to check on some rotted subroofing on the barn when I walked down to get the mail," she added. "We can start with that this afternoon."

Apparently she planned to work alongside him. Well, who was he to complain? Her proximity would be pleasant even if she had two left thumbs. Parking as directed beside a sagging, diminutive house trailer that looked as if the wind would whistle between its seams as soon as the weather turned cold, he stuffed his keys in his back pocket and took a moment to check out its interior. He rounded the barn in time to meet Holly as she emerged from the house with two tall glasses and a frosty pitcher.

The tea was cold and lemony, the way he liked it. Taking a deep draught that quenched the sensation of road dust in his throat, he paused and finished it to the last drop. "Thanks, that hit the spot," he said as he returned the glass to her.

Fastening on the carpenter's apron she handed him, he followed her up the extension ladder she'd propped against the barn. For the sake of his peace of mind, he tried not to stare at the shape of her denim-clad derriere too much.

The subroofing was rotten, as she'd said, and they had to knock out a sizable chunk of it. They were hard at work, patching the spot with fresh plywood, when another cloud of gravel dust arose in the distance.

"That'll be the school bus, dropping off Lisa," Holly said, pushing a loose strand of hair back from her forehead and scooting for the ladder. "I'll be back in a minute. I want to see how her day went."

From his perch, Jake watched as a traditional yellow school bus drew up beside the ranch gate to discharge a skinny, half-grown girl with a mass of carroty, flyaway curls. Clad in jeans, boots and a plaid flannel shirt, the child juggled a book bag, lunch pail and some sort of rolled-up art-work as she raced up the dirt track to where Holly waited by the corral for her. The enthusiastic hug they exchanged when they met caused his mouth to soften in approval.

A gangly, freckle-faced child who clearly knew herself to be well loved, Dutch's granddaughter wriggled free and held up her drawing. Watching them together, Jake was reminded of the warm way his mother had greeted him when he came home from school. Like his mom had been, Holly was a widow, struggling to hold a ranch together. At first glance, she appeared to be doing a fairly good job of it. Yet it was easy to see that mothering came first with her.

Careful, he reminded himself as he bent over his task. You can't afford to switch sides. The most you can do is see to it that she gets a fair shake.

Meanwhile, Lisa had become aware of his presence. "Who's that?" she asked.

Holly shrugged. "A man who came by this afternoon looking for work. I decided to let him help me with a few projects I need to finish before the snow flies."

Briefly continuing to squint at Jake, Lisa returned her gaze to Holly. "He doesn't look like Ernie or any of our other hired hands," she commented. "Is he going to stay?"

The question tweaked at Holly's sense of fate. Maybe he *would*. She wanted to hug herself at the thought. A moment later she was telling herself not to be ridiculous. The appealing, dark-haired cowboy who was pounding nails into her roof was nobody to her—just a passing stranger. He'd be on his way before the week was out.

"A few days at most," she answered, smoothing her stepdaughter's unruly hair as she ignored her goose bumps. "There are brownies in the cookie jar. Do you have any homework?"

Chapter Two

By 5:00 p.m., Lisa had finished studying her spelling words and completed her geography lesson. She hung over the corral fence, feeding carrots to a sprightly bay filly as she talked to it in a crooning voice. Both girl and horse seemed content with the interchange.

Glancing at her watch, Holly excused herself and climbed down the ladder to make dinner. Jake continued to hammer away until the subroofing portion of their task was complete. As he washed up afterward by the pump, he noticed Lisa watching him.

"Mighty nice filly," he said admiringly. "Is she yours?"

The girl nodded. "Her name's Comet. My dad bought her for me. He died in a rodeo accident when I was eight."

Jake wasn't quite sure what to say to that. Not responding, he finger-combed his damp hair.

"Do *you* like horses?" Lisa asked.

"Love 'em," he answered wholeheartedly, and then added a white lie, depending on whether you counted the string of saddle mares he kept at his place outside Durango. "I don't have one at the moment."

They were still talking when Holly appeared on the porch in a red denim apron to call them in to supper. She caught the tag end of Jake's comments to her stepdaughter as they approached.

"You might say horses are like people," he was saying. "They can smell it when you're afraid of them. And they'll take advantage. Some are bad eggs, not worth knowing. The good ones pay back all the trouble you have to take."

As Jake stepped inside with Lisa, his most cherished fantasies about home and hearth paled in comparison to the interior of Holly's house and the dinner she'd cooked. In contrast to the rapidly gathering dusk, her cozy living-and-kitchen area was bathed in the yellow glow of lamplight. He noted natural log walls, an island counter equipped with a gas stove and copper pots, baskets hanging from exposed overhead beams. Hand-braided rugs warmed the gleaming pine floors. A fire was crackling in her fieldstone fireplace, doubtless to ward off the evening chill.

But it was the meal itself that seized the greater part of his attention. Casually arranged on the blue-and-white patterned cloth that covered her round oak table, a trio of white ironstone serving dishes contained picture-perfect fried chicken, mashed potatoes and sweet corn on the ear. He spied a napkin-lined basket of what appeared to be flaky homemade biscuits. A blue pottery bowl held applesauce, something he hadn't eaten since he was a kid. A ravenous sensation of hunger he hadn't been aware of feeling earlier washed over him.

With a shy smile at him, Lisa slid into her place.

"You can sit here," Holly directed, motioning Jake to a chair across from the empty one that had been Clint's.

He was surprised and impressed by the moment of quiet that preceded the meal.

Apparently, it showed. "We're not what you'd call religious," Holly explained, briefly meeting his intense, blue gaze as she passed the chicken to him. "There isn't time, for one thing. But I think it's good to reflect at the end of the day on what we've accomplished, and what we're thankful for."

The drumstick Jake bit into nearly melted in his mouth. Ditto Holly's country gravy. Mostly silent as he devoured one of the best meals he'd ever eaten, he watched and listened intently as Holly and Lisa discussed what was happening on the ranch and went over her day at school. His initial judgment that they formed a close-knit family of two only deepened as the meal progressed. The question, *What can I be thinking of, stepping into their lives this way?* kept running through his head.

Pragmatic, let-the-chips-fall-where-they-may attorney that he was, he was more than a little uncomfortable deceiving Holly Yarborough. Yet from his own perspective, his presence in her house was a perfect fit. It was as if he'd been moving toward that circle of lamplight and that particular dinner table for most of his adult years, yearning for what they could give him, though he couldn't have described his lack.

Now he sensed what he'd been missing, though he still couldn't put it into words. I'll be damned if I'll walk away in the name of professional ethics, he rationalized. I have a couple of weeks, maybe even a month, at my disposal and my motive is good—checking out the kind of parenting Lisa has received. If I hadn't found them, somebody else would have. Because of my personal relationship with Dutch, I'm better equipped than they would be to ease the inevitable transition, help work out a compromise that will benefit everyone.

Of course, he realized there'd be a price to pay, whether he confessed the truth about his identity now or later. Once Holly found out who he represented, they'd find themselves on the opposite sides of a very high fence.

For her part, though she did her best not to let it show, Holly was engaged in an emotional tussle of her own. Following Clint's death, she'd vowed to devote her energies to running the ranch and raising Lisa rather than getting romantically involved with someone new. The girl's early years had been a hodgepodge of temporary abodes and shifting caretakers, exacerbated by the struggle between her unmarried parents, that could have set her on a less-than-fortuitous path. Now she had a stable home. Friends. A parent she trusted. Holly didn't plan to let anything rock the boat.

The limited array of bachelors, divorced men and widowers in Larisson Valley had made her resolve easy to keep. Now the sensual tug of a man she'd just met was threatening to undermine its foundation. Though she barely glanced at Jake throughout the meal, she was acutely aware of his scrutiny, his energizing but disturbing male presence.

It was Lisa's turn to clear the table and do the dishes, together with any pans that hadn't already been washed during the cooking process. To Holly's surprise, as she sat down at her desk to go through the afternoon mail, Jake volunteered to help. With Lisa washing while he wielded a dish towel, they made short work of the task, laughing and talking as they went.

He has a natural affinity for kids, she decided, watching them. Plainly captivated by so much attention from a fascinating stranger, the girl was recounting an incident that had taken place on her school playground earlier that week, and asking Jake's advice. She misses her father, but it's more than that, Holly knew. Like me, she's hungry for the presence of a man in the house. There are some kinds of support only a nurturing male influence can provide for a girl.

However likable and friendly he might be, no temporary hired man could fill that gap for Lisa. A genuine father figure was needed. Sighing, Holly affixed stamps to the couple of envelopes she'd addressed and got to her feet. "I'm going to take these out to the mailbox," she announced. "I'll be back in a moment."

"Can I call Jane when I'm finished with the dishes?" Lisa asked.

"Provided you keep the conversation to half an hour. You need to spend some time on your science project, remember."

Her stepdaughter nodded dutifully. "Okay."

By now, it was fully dark. The night was clear, lit by a quarter moon and what seemed a billion stars. Walking to the mailbox and back—a half-mile jaunt—freed Holly of some of the sexual tension that had been bothering her. She fully expected that, by the time she returned, Jake would have left the house for his temporary digs. To her chagrin, he was waiting for her in the porch shadows.

"Could we talk for a moment?" he asked, gazing down at her from his six-foot height as he leaned against one of the rough pine columns that supported the roof.

His speech was awfully cultivated for an itinerant ranch laborer. "I guess so," she conceded, waving him to one of the split-ash rockers and taking the other. "What about?"

Jake cleared his throat. "I glanced inside the trailer where I'm supposed to sleep before going to work on the barn, and I couldn't help noticing that your former hired man cleared out lock, stock and barrel," he said. "To all appearances, he's gone for good. I was wondering if—provided my work is satisfactory—I could have his job on a more permanent basis."

In Holly's view, he was rushing things. Yet she couldn't argue his point. She needed him. Unfortunately, she'd barely been able to scrape up Ernie Townsend's minimal wages from week to week. At the moment, her budget was so strained that even that late, unlamented hireling's stipend was beyond her means.

"I can't afford to pay you much more than we agreed on for temporary work," she hedged. "At most, sixty dollars a week. Plus lodging and all the food you can eat. From what little I've seen, you're a hard and capable worker. You could do a lot better than that someplace else."

Jake thought how much he enjoyed sitting there, rocking on the porch with her. He wondered if she'd let him get to know her better. "I like it here," he said with a quixotic shrug. "Money isn't everything. With nobody but myself to think about, I can afford to be choosy, I guess."

It sounded as if they had a deal. "All right, if that's how you feel about it," she responded, stifling the misgivings that arose from her lack of knowledge of him. She hoped her strong attraction to him wouldn't plague her too much.

"I like to get an early start," she added, daring to hope he wouldn't quit after a couple of weeks as so many others had, though she almost wished he would. "Breakfast's at 6:30 a.m., so Lisa and I can have plenty of time to eat and talk before she catches the bus."

As Jake's sojourn at Honeycomb Ranch neared the end of its first week, Holly found herself waking up each morning with growing apprehension and excitement. Thursday was no exception. Burrowing for several drowsy seconds beneath the smooth cotton top sheet, patchwork quilt and down comforter that graced her four-poster bed, she stretched and yawned, testing the heightened body awareness his presence in her life had evoked. A voyager returned unwillingly from her travels, she clung to the tattered remnants of dreams that drifted through her head.

That most of the dreams had been about Jake, she had little doubt. She'd remembered snatches of them, in which she and her dark-haired, sexy hired man had gone exploring in the north pasture on horseback, or tumbled into the hayloft and, accidentally, each other's arms.

Disturbing to her peace of mind once she was fully awake, they had a tenuous foothold in reality, she guessed. Once their roofing project was completed, she and Jake had begun the lengthy task of replacing fence posts and stringing fresh barbed wire along Honeycomb's north boundary. They'd also spent an afternoon forking several truckloads of hay into the barn for winter use.

Whatever work they happened to be doing seemed to occasion physical closeness. Now and then, there was a brush of actual contact. The day before, after removing her gloves to eat a sandwich from the brown-bag lunch they'd carried with them, she'd reached for a hammer and collided with his hand. The air between them had fairly crackled with electricity as their eyes had met and held. For what had seemed aeons, she'd felt herself drowning in lake blue depths.

According to her windup alarm, it was 6:00 a.m. Time to get up, throw on some clothes and make breakfast. She could hear Lisa puttering about in the next room, getting ready for school. Before long, Jake would come whistling in the door.

His presence in our lives has forced me to remember that I'm a woman, with fantasies and a need to be touched, she conceded, throwing back the covers and sliding barefoot onto the cool board floor beside her bed. Until he appeared, I was satisfied with ranching and mothering. Now it's not enough. All the same, she had responsibilities. She didn't plan to let things get out of hand with him.

Having showered and washed her hair the night before, she needed less than a minute to shimmy into underwear, jeans, a turtleneck and a plaid flannel shirt. Her feet were quickly encased in woolen socks and cowboy boots. A few licks from her hairbrush and the long, blond hair she could almost sit on was smooth and gleaming. Plaiting it in its customary braid, she hesitated before the round, oak-framed mirror above her dresser. She didn't usually wear makeup. Yet maybe a little lipstick wouldn't hurt....

She was dishing up oatmeal, scrambled eggs, ham, cinnamon rolls and warm fruit compote when Jake rapped lightly at the door and sauntered in. "Hi, sunshine," he greeted Lisa, taking what had quickly become "his" seat at the table. "Morning, Miz Yarborough. It's a little bit nippy out there today."

Soon the aspens would be past their peak. The year was turning downward, toward winter, the loneliest season of all on a ranch when you didn't have someone to love. "All the more reason to keep after that fencing," Holly retorted and then wished she hadn't spoken so brusquely. To date, Jake McKenzie had behaved like a perfect gentlemen. The least she could do was make polite conversation with him.

Seemingly oblivious to any lapse of cordiality on her part, Jake helped himself from the steaming array of serving dishes and dug in. "These eggs are done just right," he commented.

"Thank you." Aware it was for his benefit she'd put on lipstick that morning and begun cooking elaborate meals on a daily basis for the first time since Clint's death, Holly bit into a piece of toast.

It seemed Lisa had noticed the changes, too. "Know what, Holly?" she asked suddenly. "You've been fixing cowboy breakfasts ever since Jake came, the way you used to do for Daddy."

The innocent observation caused Holly's cheeks to flush. She couldn't avoid the quizzical look Jake shot in her direction. "I *did* promise you good food as part of your wages," she told him a trifle defensively.

He grinned, the deepening laugh lines that bracketed his mouth devastating in their attractiveness. "Nobody can say you haven't delivered," he assured her in his smoky voice.

A moment later, she was off the hook. The conversation had turned to a problem Lisa was having with one of her classmates at school. "Every afternoon while we're waiting for the bus, Tommy Danzig grabs my book bag and runs off with it," the girl complained, glancing from Holly to Jake and back again. "Jane and some of my other friends try to help me chase him. But it doesn't do any good. I never get my stuff back until the very last second. I'm always afraid Tommy will dump it in the creek or something, and I'll get blamed for wrecking my schoolbooks."

As befitted his lack of standing, Jake remained silent, waiting for Holly to speak.

"Have you told Mrs. Allen about it?" she asked, referring to the girl's fifth-grade teacher.

Lisa shook her head.

"Maybe you should, sweetheart."

"I don't want to be a tattletale," Lisa protested.

As Holly poured more coffee without advancing an alternative solution, Jake decided to put in his two cents' worth. "You might have to take your mom's advice if the problem keeps up," he said diffidently. "But maybe there's something else you could try first. It sounds to me like that boy wants your attention, not your books. If you stop giving it to him—just shrug your shoulders and turn your back when he runs off with your stuff—all the fun will go out of his little game. He might just give up without a fight, and quit bothering you.''

It was light out by the time they finished breakfast. A short time later, the bus was collecting Lisa at the ranch gate. Having trucked enough fencing supplies up to the north pasture the previous afternoon to last them through that day's labor, Holly and Jake decided to make the trip on horseback. Clearing the table and putting the dishes in to soak while he fed the chickens and readied the horses, she met him a few minutes later by the corral.

He'd saddled Brandy, her paint, and Clint's chestnut, Dasher, for himself. "Let me give you a hand," he offered. *Thanks, I don't need it* was on the tip of her tongue. Instead she responded with a simple, "Thank you," and accepted an assist into the saddle.

Jake didn't need anyone to tell him that his display of manners was partly an excuse to touch her. He couldn't seem to keep his hand from brushing negligently against hers as he handed her the reins. God, but she was good to look at—all gold, pewter and honey with that corn-silk hair and those big, gray eyes, her tanned but dewy skin. He kept wanting to touch her and being forced to stay his hand.

Yet she didn't wear makeup except for the modest touch of lipstick he'd noticed for the first time that morning. Had she put it on for him? More smitten with Holly than he'd been with anyone for as long as he could remember, he could only speculate.

As they headed out, with Holly leading the way toward the foothills of the San Juan Mountains, which bordered her ranch to the north, he gave the chestnut its head. Instead of drinking in the scenery, his gaze was riveted to the compact bounce of Holly's seat in the saddle, the way her slim, denim-clad thighs gripped the sides of her mount. Red-blooded male that he was, he couldn't help but wonder how it would feel to have those thighs gripping him.

But it wasn't just looks and a dynamite figure that drew him to Holly Yarborough. Nor was it the kind of sexy, sophisticated teasing most of the women he'd dated had mastered so well. From what he could determine, she was far too genuine to play that kind of game. When she laughed and teased, he guessed, her laughter would come straight from the heart.

Silently leading the way, Holly reflected that the fencing project was much larger than she'd anticipated. Aside from the work they'd done on the barn and checking on her herd, they'd spent most of their time just trying to make a dent in it. I'll need Jake till the middle of November, at least, she thought. And realized her concern over securing her pastures wasn't her only motive for thinking so.

The tall grass of the north pasture was still damp from the passage of rainy weather the night before—the day bright and breezy, cool enough to require a jacket as they set to work. In the distance, swift-moving, patchy clouds skimmed snowcapped peaks. Intense drifts of aspen shimmered like yellow fire on the lower slopes.

"Beautiful up here, isn't it?" Holly said as they paused to share the steaming hot coffee she'd packed in a thermos.

"You bet." Jake's endorsement resonated with the emphasis of sincerity. He wanted to add, *So are you,* but held his tongue. He doubted if that kind of compliment would improve his standing with her very much.

"Is it anything like Idaho?"

"Quite a bit. The peace of it settles into a man's empty places."

Even as he spoke, Jake could feel himself relaxing a little more from the heady, high-wire atmosphere of his lawyer's existence. With each day he spent at Honeycomb, it seemed, he moved deeper into Holly Yarborough's simple but satisfying life of physical labor, fresh air and mountain vistas, and further away from the commitment that had brought him to her door. Annoyed that it should have arisen, he deliberately pushed all consideration of the conflict loyalty to his client was sure to generate from his head. *If I have anything to say about it,* he thought, *for the next month or so I'll live in the present tense.*

Sipping her coffee as she regarded him, Holly puzzled over what kind of man he was. He certainly didn't talk like your average ranch hand or a common drifter. Was he running from the law? Or some scandal in his past? A terrible failure or blot on his record? Supposedly he'd grown up on a ranch and his familiarity with the work seemed to back up his claim. *Maybe he inherited the one where he lived as a boy,* she speculated, *and lost his shirt. Unless she learned how to make cattle pay, and quickly, the same fate would unfold for them.*

Meanwhile, the chemistry between them was strong. Mesmerized by the mystery of Jake's past almost as much as she was the strong sexual energy that emanated from him, she lectured herself that it would be crazy to succumb. God knew what kind of historical baggage had arrived with the man in his dusty red truck. Yet the fact remained that she sorely wanted him.

Even a temporary fling was out of the question. For one thing, lovemaking outside of marriage was against her principles. For another, she had Lisa to think about.

That night at the supper table, her redheaded stepdaughter had news for them. She'd tried Jake's suggestion about how to handle Tommy Danzig and, to her astonishment, it had worked.

"When Tommy did his thing, I just looked at Jane and shrugged," she reported with a pleased and satisfied air. "We turned our backs on him and walked in the opposite direction. After a minute or two he followed us and shoved my stuff at me. 'Here's your dumb old book bag—I don't want it, anyway,' he said. Jane and I just laughed at him. He looked awfully..."

She hesitated, casting about for the proper word.

"Sheepish?" Jake suggested.

Lisa nodded. "*Right.* I don't think he'll bother me again. If he does, I'll tell everyone it's because he likes me. And that'll *totally* embarrass him."

"Sounds like a winner," Jake said.

I'd never have thought of advising her to do what Jake did, Holly admitted to herself as she watched them exchange self-congratulatory grins. Yet, as a former teacher, I'm supposed to be an expert in handling schoolyard confrontations. Apparently her new ranch laborer had a gift for strategy in addition to his ability to entrance females of all ages. It was clear Lisa thought so.

With each day that passed, Holly's stepdaughter and the dark-haired cowboy who'd taken up residence in her hired man's trailer seemed to cement their growing friendship a little further. I shouldn't find it so surprising, Holly thought. Lisa needs a father figure. In the absence of one, she probably can't help latching onto the first charming stranger who takes an interest in her.

Maybe that's what *she* was guilty of—daydreaming about Jake because he was the only man available. But she couldn't get the explanation to stick. Slipping on her down parka, she went outside to sit on the porch while Jake and Lisa finished washing and drying the supper dishes. Huddled in her jacket, she gazed at the chilly, star-filled evening and tried to decide what to do. Firing him was out of the question. He didn't deserve it. Besides, she needed him too much.

Hugging herself against the cold but unwilling to go back inside until he and Lisa were finished, she jumped a little as he came out on the porch and asked if he could sit a spell.

They were co-workers in addition to being employer and employee. Plus they ate all their meals together. "Be my guest," she heard herself answering him.

He was wearing his lightweight denim jacket over a ragged sweater and flannel shirt, and suddenly she worried that it wasn't warm enough. "Some of my late husband's things are still boxed up in the attic," she revealed. "I'm sure there are several winter parkas in the mix. Clint was tall, like you. If you'd like one of them, I'm sure it would fit...."

Touched by her generosity, Jake reached across the space that separated them to pat her hand. "Thanks, but I have one of my own in the truck," he said.

The sensation of his skin against hers was electric for both of them. To cover her response before it could lead to something even more unsettling, Holly changed the subject. "You said you were born and raised on a ranch in Idaho," she reminded him. "Was it your parents' place? Why'd you leave it?"

Abruptly, she was prying into his past. Well, he'd expected it at some point. He realized he'd have to tread carefully. "Vietnam," he answered, letting the single word stand in for his experience in that once-tortured country.

"You were there."

"During the last days of the war, as an eighteen-year-old medic's assistant."

She was silent a moment, digesting the information. So that's where some of his self-possession comes from, she thought. Maybe even some of his rootlessness. "You didn't go back to Idaho afterward?" she asked.

He'd try to give her the straight scoop on his life insofar as he could. "Not for long," he answered. "Mom passed away of cancer a few months after my return. The ranch was sold to cover her debts."

Apparently, his mother had faced a good deal of trouble keeping her head above water as a rancher, just as Holly did. For some reason, the revelation made her feel closer to him.

"I'm sorry," she said simply.

"It was some years back. I'm over it."

"What about your dad? Where was he when all this was taking place?"

"He died of a heart attack when I was eleven."

Jake's early history had paralleled Lisa's, with the exception that his mother, not a stepparent, had finished the job of raising him. But that didn't explain the life he'd chosen for himself.

"Once the ranch was sold, you hit the road...opted for the life of a traveling cowpoke, is that it?" she asked, trying to understand. "Didn't you ever want to settle down? Get an education and a decent job? Maybe even buy a place of your own?"

He'd have to lie or answer her question with a question. He supposed that was the price of his quest to find Dutch's granddaughter. By now, of course, it had become something far more complex.

"What's wrong with traveling around, working only when you choose or necessity forces you to?" he parried. "You see a lot of pretty country...meet some mighty interesting people that way."

She didn't reply and for several minutes neither of them said anything further as they rocked and listened to the cries of migrating geese that were seeking nighttime cover.

By portraying himself as a drifter, Jake decided, he'd been truthful in a larger sense. He *had* been drifting for quite a while—from one legal victory to another without being fired up by any of them...and from woman to woman without finding love. Ironically, by the act of seeking what *would* matter to him he'd placed it beyond his grasp.

"Tell me about you," he said. "Where did you grow up?"

Holly shrugged. "There isn't much to tell. I'm a native of northern New Mexico. I've lived there most of my life, with the exception of the four years I've spent here and another two in Alaska. My parents took a fling at homesteading when I was Lisa's age. Or perhaps I should say my father did. We went against my mother's wishes. He was determined to make his fortune on the last frontier."

"And did he?"

She shook her head. "We came back poorer than when we left. To make matters worse, his insistence that we move had soured their relationship. They divorced shortly after our return to New Mexico."

So she knew what it was to be the child of warring parents. Maybe that was why she'd tried so hard to make a home for her late husband's little girl...and done a damn fine job of it, in his opinion.

"What brought you here, to Larisson Valley?" he asked. "Ranching's not a common occupation for a single woman."

"As you must have guessed from my remark about the clothes, if you hadn't earlier, I'm a widow," she replied. "Lisa and I didn't get into ranching on our own. When we bought this place, her father was still with us."

Gently, Jake pressed her to elaborate. He wanted to hear the story from her point of view.

Leaving out Dawn Hargrett's identity and making no mention of Lisa's grandparents, Holly told him about teaching school, meeting and marrying Clint and becoming her pupil Lisa's stepmother. Clint's lottery winnings, his dream of ranching and his fear that Lisa's mother would try to reclaim her as he lay dying were among the things she related.

It was only when she'd finished that she stopped to ask herself if she'd told a stranger too much, and wonder what had prompted her to do so. She only hoped she hadn't extended a clue to their whereabouts through him to someone who knew the Hargretts. She supposed the likelihood of that was minimal.

As he'd listened, Jake had been forced to admit her perspective on who ought to be raising Lisa had considerable merit. Dawn *was* a threat to the stability of the girl's upbringing. It was also becoming increasingly clear that to cut Lisa off from Holly would be to separate her from the only mother she could remember.

Now, sensing the discomfort betrayed by her silence, Jake attempted to minimize it by changing the subject. "You have to wonder what brings two people from different backgrounds and beginnings to the same dot on the map so they can share their journeys," he mused. "Take you and me, for instance. The odds of us meeting were slim to nonexistent. And yet we did."

Holly wasn't sure how to answer him. She only knew he'd raised a lot of questions in her head, at a time when she needed to focus unswervingly on raising Lisa and paying her bills.

"I couldn't begin to tell you," she answered, getting to her feet. "Meanwhile, it's getting colder by the minute out here. I'd better say good-night."

With the cultivated manners that had her questioning his claim to be a drifter, Jake got up, too. Suddenly they were standing very close together. Holly's pulse seemed to flutter in her throat. Overwhelmed by the stab of desire his nearness evoked, she was rooted to the spot. She doubted if she could move or speak.

His six-foot-plus frame looming in shadow against the moonlit backdrop of the yard, Jake gazed down at her. How lovely she is, he thought. And how innocent—seemingly untouched, though she was a married woman. With all that was masculine in him, he longed to enfold her, press his mouth against hers.

He almost lost it when her lips parted as if in anticipation. Raising his hands as if to grasp her and pull her to him, he quickly dropped them again. She gave a little sigh, betrayed by a plume of frosty breath.

"Good night, Miz Yarborough. See you in the morning." Giving her his customary salute, Jake headed for his trailer.

As she watched him go, Holly told herself to be grateful for her narrow escape. Simultaneously, she continued to puzzle over the mystery he represented. Though he wore threadbare clothes, knew ranching and had work-roughened hands, Jake McKenzie was smart and—she was willing to bet—educated, not to mention the sexiest man she'd ever met. What was he doing at Honeycomb, upsetting her emotional applecart while he worked for peanuts?

Chapter Three

Going inside, Holly sat down at her sewing machine to finish a corduroy skirt she was making for Lisa. Before long, she was ready to fit it on the girl in front of an oval pier glass that stood to one side of her sewing area. Her pincushion at the ready, she made several adjustments to her handiwork and then set about stitching them into place as her stepdaughter went back to reading her new Judy Blume novel in a nearby chair.

Though she did her best to concentrate on the task at hand, she couldn't seem to get Jake McKenzie and her attraction to him out of her head. A half hour later, she placed the skirt atop her workbasket to be hemmed the following evening. "Time to put the book away and get ready for bed, Leez," she said.

"Okay, Holly." With a hug and kiss that plainly indicated Holly's affection for her was mutual, Lisa trooped off to do her bidding.

Still aching for Jake's kiss and in the mood for some pampering, Holly decided to draw herself a bath and have a good, long soak as soon as Lisa was finished in the bathroom.

A few minutes later, Lisa had completed the nightly routine of brushing her teeth, washing her face and putting on her pajamas. "Okay if I read another chapter?" she coaxed. "I'll do it under the covers so if I get tired I can just turn out the light."

Sometimes Lisa reminded Holly of herself at the same age. She smiled indulgently. "You sold me, pumpkin. Another fifteen minutes."

Changing to a light blue chenille robe that was slightly oversized on her slender frame, Holly went into the bathroom and ran a tub full of scented bubbles. She even lit a couple of candles and turned on the portable radio she kept on a shelf below the medicine cabinet. She was about to drop the robe and slide into the suds when she thought she heard Lisa calling her. Though it turned out that she was mistaken, she decided to leave the door open partway, just in case.

"Ahh," she murmured, sinking into a mound of bubbles that billowed to her chin. "This is pure indulgence."

No doubt the heated water and subtle scent of her bubble bath were part and parcel with her sensuous stretching when she awoke from her early-morning dreams—second-class substitutes for lying warm and cosseted in Jake's arms. Well, what if they are? she reasoned as the strains of one of her favorite movie themes filled the air. They're good for what ails me . . . and a whole lot more sensible than the alternative.

Outside in his trailer, which was cramped, chilly and lonely, Jake was restless with unacted desire. Try as he would, he couldn't get his thoughts to quit running in circles. You should have kissed her when you had the chance, he scolded himself. You know you wanted to. Right, his sensible side responded in a sarcastic tone. And get hustled off the property. I didn't realize you were ready to leave just yet.

The fact of the matter was, he wanted to see her again. *Tonight.*

With a little rush of satisfaction and energy, he recalled their need to get additional rolls of barbed wire from town before they could continue with their fencing project. On the way, they could drop Lisa off at school. She'd get a kick out of it, and they wouldn't have to get up so early. Deciding to use the reminder as an excuse to talk to Holly right then, he put on his jacket.

Several lamps were still lit as Jake approached the house. When rapping lightly at the door didn't bring an answer, he tried it and found it unlocked. After a moment's hesitation, he entered. The kitchen and living areas were deserted. However, a radio was playing, probably in one of the bedrooms. Somebody was still up.

Glancing toward the pier glass where Holly had fitted and pinned up the hem of Lisa's skirt, Jake sucked in his breath. By chance, the mirror was positioned at just the right angle to the open bathroom door to give back Holly's reflection as she got out of the tub. She's like Venus rising from the sea, he thought, his body responding with swift desire.

God but she was beautiful to him! A soft pink against the creamy flesh tones of her skin, her nipples stood erect from the bath and colder air of the room as she patted the last traces of bubble bath from her body. Unconfined in its usual braid, her glorious Scandinavian-blond hair formed a wavy, damp halo about her head and shoulders. Jake couldn't help noticing that the patch of coarser curls between her thighs was the same Nordic shade.

"What are you doing, Jake?" Lisa's voice asked, causing him to jump with a guilty start.

Aware Lisa was up, Holly wrapped her towel more closely about her body and shut the bathroom door to finish drying herself.

Meanwhile, Lisa was waiting for an answer. "You saw Holly without any clothes on," she accused in a low voice. "You were staring at her in the mirror."

His arousal mercifully having subsided, Jake turned to face the girl. "I didn't mean to," he replied. "It just happened."

Clearly Lisa wasn't buying the explanation. "The way you were looking at her," she persisted, condemnation in her tone. "It wasn't right."

Jake knew he had to do something—fast—or there'd be hell to pay, not just for his own sake, but for the girl's. Sitting down on the arm of the chair where Lisa had been reading earlier, so that they were about the same height, he met her censure face-to-face.

"You're too young to understand fully," he said, keenly aware he was short on experience when it came to interpreting adult feelings to children. "But I'll try to explain. To a grown man, the female body is a work of beauty. I wasn't spying on Holly. But, when I saw her like that, I felt admiration. And great reverence."

It wasn't the whole truth, but it was true. For Lisa it seemed to be enough. "Okay," she said, granting him unspoken absolution. "I guess I get it."

With a sigh of relief, Jake tried to hurry her back to bed.

"What's reverence, exactly?" she demanded, prolonging the moment.

So this is what it would be like to have a kid of my own, Jake thought. He kind of liked the notion. "An attitude of honor and respect," he answered. "I honor and respect

Holly. By the way, I came back to tell her we need to get more fencing first thing in the morning. I thought we could drive you to school on the way, if that's all right with her.''

Jake was gone when Holly emerged from the bathroom a few minutes later with her robe knotted about her waist. But she'd heard his voice. She knew he'd been in the house. She wanted to know what had been going on. "What was Jake doing here?" she inquired from the doorway of Lisa's room.

Back in bed, with her down coverlet and one of Holly's grandmother's quilts pulled up to her chin, Lisa passed on Jake's message about the ride to school and the fencing.

Holly wasn't satisfied. Though to her knowledge he hadn't been standing opposite the bathroom door, something in Lisa's eyes confirmed that there was more to tell.

"What else should I know about this?" she prodded.

Lisa blinked. "I thought I heard someone come in. When I got up to see, he was watching you dry off...in the mirror.''

Goose bumps of desire and excitement raced over Holly's skin even as outrage swelled in her breast. With her stepdaughter gauging her reaction, she tried to quell them both.

"You mean...he was just standing there, staring at me?" she asked.

Lisa nodded. "When I asked him what he was doing, he said he didn't mean to spy on you. That he saw you by accident. He said a grown man thinks a woman's body is beautiful. That he looks at it with respect...I mean, reverence. 'I honor and respect Holly,' he said.''

Awash in conflicting emotions, Holly couldn't seem to find the right words to answer her.

"Did Jake do something wrong?" Lisa asked worriedly.

"Not intentionally," Holly said, certain Jake couldn't have known she was bathing and unwilling the girl should get the wrong message from what had occurred. "It was just an accident. I should have locked the outside door."

As she put on her nightgown and climbed into bed, Holly had to admit the tenor of Jake's explanation to Lisa had hinted at a basic decency on his part. Unfortunately, it also confirmed that he found her attractive. With everything that was womanly in her, she longed to bask in his admiration, taste the pleasure of nestling naked in his arms.

His remarks further strengthened her impression that he was very sophisticated for a cowboy. Though Clint had been capable of similar emotions, he wouldn't have been able to articulate them that way. Who *is* Jake McKenzie? she asked herself for the second time that evening as she switched off her bedside lamp. And what does he want from me? Though she had some idea how to respond to the latter question, she'd begun to feel a full-fledged answer to the former might shake her to her roots.

Man-woman tension between Jake and Holly over what she'd mentally dubbed "the bathtub incident" was at its zenith the following morning as they dropped Lisa off at school, bought the wire and a few other supplies and returned to work on the ranch. Her worst moments came when she met his eyes as she welcomed him to the breakfast table and, later, as they drove her stepdaughter to Beamish Elementary in Larisson. Jake had offered to take the wheel. To her chagrin, she'd found herself wedged between him and Lisa, because the girl was getting out first. Thanks to the limited space in the cab of her truck, their denim-clad thighs were pressed tightly together.

At the feed-and-hardware store, which was her source of wire, she noticed the proprietor, sixty-two-year-old Harlan Matthews, eyeing them speculatively. *You never brought any of them other fellas who worked for you into town,* his raised eyebrows seemed to suggest. *This one's smooth...and just the right age. Anythin' goin' on?* By afternoon, she suspected, the valley's party lines would be humming with gossip about them.

She was quiet, almost morose, as they returned to Honeycomb and bounced up a rutted dirt track that led to their current work site along the north boundary. Finally, unable to stomach the way she was hugging the passenger door and answering his conversational gambits in monosyllables any longer, Jake apologized to her.

"I gather Lisa told you I intruded on your privacy last night," he said, casting a swift, blue-eyed glance in her direction as he drove. "I want you to know I'm sorry...that it was in no way deliberate on my part."

Trapped by his forthrightness and gentlemanly request for her pardon, Holly had no choice but to grant the forgiveness he sought. "As a matter of fact, she did tell me," she admitted, thawing noticeably. "Let's forget it, okay? There wasn't any harm done. I never thought you came back to ogle me on purpose."

They both knew he'd have looked his fill if Lisa hadn't discovered him. Nevertheless, as a result of clearing the air, things were more comfortable between them as they set to work. I doubt if it was a big deal to him the way it was to me, Holly thought as she unrolled a length of wire and held it taut so Jake could hammer it to one of the fence posts. With his looks and come-hither personality, he's probably seen more naked women than he can count.

They were interacting a bit more easily by the time Lisa rushed to greet them on their return to the barn at the end of the workday.

The girl was practically jumping out of her skin with excitement. "Holly...Jake! Look at this!" she exclaimed, waving a flyer, which she eagerly handed to her step-mother.

The flyer, a bit crumpled from being stuffed in Lisa's book bag, had been distributed at her school that after-noon to remind valley residents about the annual Larisson Valley Fall Dance. Traditionally involving mostly square dancing, though there were ballroom numbers, too, it would be held a week from the upcoming Saturday, at the hay barn on the Cunningham ranch. Three years ago, Clint, Holly and Lisa had attended as a family, and he'd waltzed his daughter around the room. Holly knew it was a big deal—one of the girl's fondest memories.

As she read the flyer and passed it to Jake, her step-daughter was jumping up and down impatiently. "Can we go?" she begged. "*Please, please, please!* Since Dad died, it's been all work and no play for us. It's time we had a lit-tle fun!"

Though part of her recognized the truth of Lisa's state-ment and longed to say yes, Holly hesitated. The prospect of sitting on the sidelines for most of the evening with the valley's elderly, widowed population wasn't a very appeal-ing one. "I don't know, Leez..." she answered, feeling a little selfish.

"You know you want to! Jake can come along so you'll have somebody to dance with. Right, Jake?"

While he might enjoy gazing at her naked form if the op-portunity arose, in Holly's opinion, Jake probably had a woman or two stashed away for whenever he was in need of loving. He wouldn't want to waste time dancing attendance on his prissy employer, who couldn't be beguiled into the sack.

"Naturally, your free time is your own," she murmured, giving him a rueful look. "I wouldn't dream of impos-ing...."

"I'm not much of a dancer. But I'll be happy to go if Holly wants me to," he told Lisa, cutting off her excuse at the knees.

"Then it's settled!" Lisa was exuberant.

Holly shook her head. "Not so fast. I haven't decided yet."

Washing up at the pump, Jake strained his ears to hear their conversation as they turned and walked together toward the house. To his way of thinking, Holly didn't need him to dance with her. If there were any red-blooded men alive and well in Larisson Valley, she wouldn't lack for partners.

When he joined them a short time later at the table for a dinner of flaky biscuits, homemade chili, cabbage slaw and warm chocolate-chip cake, he gathered Holly hadn't made a commitment yet. With a bit of questioning by her stepmother, Lisa confessed the reason for her unbridled enthusiasm during the meal. She had a crush on one of her schoolmates.

"Not Tommy Danzig?" Holly teased, naming the former book-bag thief.

The girl wrinkled her nose. "It wouldn't be Tommy if he was the last boy in the world."

"Who, then?"

"Promise not to tell *anyone?* It's Jason Cunningham. Don't you think he's cute?"

Watching them together, Jake remarked to himself what a good stepmother Holly was. Without fanfare, she invested herself in things like fully engaged conversation and making Lisa's favorite desserts. It was easy to see the girl felt pampered and loved, even on a shoestring budget. It occurred to him that his blond employer was a lot like his late mother, whom he'd greatly admired. Funny, but the comparison didn't stop him from wanting her.

Unable to get a firm answer from Holly about attending the dance, Lisa turned to wheedling Jake. He promptly repeated his willingness to go, but claimed he didn't know how to dance. "I'm just an ignorant cowpoke," he said with a grin. "If I tried to dance with Holly, I'd step on her toes."

Lisa shook her head in mock disgust. "What you guys need is *practice*," she muttered inelegantly, her mouth full of cake as she jumped up to switch on the radio and turn the dial to a country-music station.

With Lisa's encouragement, while the girl did the dishes, Holly allowed Jake to sharpen his supposedly nonexistent dancing skills by dancing with her. At first they practiced square-dance moves. Though Jake pretended confusion and clumsiness, Holly had the strong impression he was bluffing.

Then the program's deejay aired an oldie known as the "Tennessee Waltz," and Jake took her in his arms. "I think maybe I could dance to this one," he whispered in his rough, deep voice.

For Holly, the sensation of being held in Jake's arms— even under such far-from-compromising circumstances— was dizzyingly erotic. Her cozy, familiar surroundings seemed to recede in soft focus, like the background elements in a romantic film. Only peripherally was she aware of Lisa pausing with a dish towel and serving platter in her hands to stand and stare at them.

Though she was sorely out of practice, somehow her feet managed to follow Jake's lead. Her left hand resting on the hard but vibrant muscles of his shoulder through the thin barrier of his worn plaid shirt, while her right was firmly grasped by warm, callused fingers, she caught a subtle whiff of after-shave she'd have sworn didn't come from the five-and-dime.

Every neuron in her body was firing at peak intensity as if she was experiencing *her* first crush. Instead, she feared, she was taking part in the first scary-sweet moves of a full-blown love affair. It was a relief, if something of a letdown, when the number came to an end and the station's announcer cut to several advertisements.

"Thank you, ma'am," Jake remarked, making her a courtly little bow as he relinquished her.

With Lisa still watching them, Holly struggled to maintain her cool. "My pleasure," she answered.

He gave her one of his bad-boy grins. "Waltzin' in the kitchen can be kind of fun," he allowed.

"But it's not the first time, is it? That you've waltzed, I mean...in the kitchen or otherwise."

The laugh lines beside his mouth deepened. "Not quite," he admitted, inviting her to share his amusement at being caught posturing. "But I can honestly say I've never enjoyed it as much."

"Ah-hem!" Loudly clearing her throat, Lisa made a bid for their attention. "So...are we going to go or what?" she asked, tilting her curly red head to one side. "According to the flyer, we have to let the Cunninghams know this weekend."

Though Holly drew out the moment as much as possible, she knew when she was licked. "I suppose we could," she answered.

"Yesss!" Abandoning her task, Lisa threw her arms around Holly's neck. "My turn to practice with Jake," she announced excitedly. "When I danced with Daddy, my feet didn't touch the ground."

Holly laughed. "That's because he was carrying you, pumpkin."

Volunteering to finish the dishes while Lisa took a turn around the room with Jake, she kept an eye on the proceedings. She couldn't help but admire the way her tall hired hand gently instructed the girl in all the right moves while continuing to pretend a lack of expertise.

At Lisa's insistence, Holly and Jake danced together again before they said good-night, so she could watch and pick up some additional pointers. Afterward, on the way from the house to his less agreeable digs behind the barn, Jake paused and leaned against one of the oversize, nearly bare cottonwood trees that shaded the yard. Holly hadn't bothered to draw the living-room curtains. He could see her and Lisa moving about in the yellow lamp glow.

This is what I've needed, he thought, an expression of longing coming over his face. Hard work and pleasantly tired muscles from working on a ranch that's not a rich man's plaything. Open country. Stars to gaze at undimmed by city lights. A pretty, decent woman to get slowly, sweetly under my skin. Just to let time unfurl and nature do its handiwork.

He wasn't ready, yet, to think about the sad truth that the pretty, decent woman who consumed his thoughts and made him want something more than a passing fling with her would probably refuse even to speak with him when she learned why he'd sought her out.

The remainder of the week passed in a blur of effort and anticipation. Meanwhile, the weather had turned warmer, ushering in a final burst of Indian summer. Already, in the foothills, the aspens were loosing showers of gold doubloons with every breeze, while at higher elevations, they stood amid the dark green winter sentinels of ponderosa pine like slender, naked ghosts.

On Friday evening, to rein in Lisa's excess energy and give her something to do while they waited for the dance to roll around, Holly floated a dinner-table suggestion. What about a picnic? They could take the horses, head a little way up into the foothills. When Lisa promptly invited Jake, she had to admit that was just what she'd been hoping would occur.

"You needn't go if you'd rather not," she told him perversely, unwilling to seem too eager. "As we agreed, Saturday afternoons and Sundays are your days off. I know this country like the back of my hand. We'll be fine, just the two of us."

As Lisa flung her a killing look, Jake considered her statement. Was she simply trying to be fair to him? Or attempting to slow the progress of a relationship that was getting too sticky for her taste? Whatever the case, he didn't plan to humor her.

"I haven't been on a picnic since I was eight," he responded. "I accept your invitation."

They left shortly before noon the following day, after seeing to it that the chickens and other livestock were cared for. As they wound up the cottonwood-lined creek, picking their way among boulders, fallen tree branches and the occasional low-lying, muddy pool, a rolled-up, Indian-patterned blanket was tied behind Holly's saddle. Beside Jake, Dasher lugged a hamper of sandwiches, potato salad, cookies and fruit, plus a thermos each of coffee and lemonade.

With Holly in the lead, astride Brandy, and Lisa following on Comet, Jake brought up the rear. Energized by the prospect of getting to know Holly better, he whistled in his contentment. None of them were related by blood or marriage. Yet it's as if we're mother, father and daughter, he thought.

Though it was cool enough that they required light jackets, the day was heartrendingly beautiful, especially in light of the fact that winter was just a few weeks away. Overhead, the sky's azure bosom provided ample pasture for flocks of fluffy white clouds. Leaves rustled as they skittered over the loose stones beneath their horses' hooves, and blew across their path like the omens of snowflakes.

Before long, the first real snow would fly, grainy as soap powder, dusting the hay bales and settling on Holly's windowsills. Would Jake be gone by then? she wondered. Would she have just her memories of him?

As they climbed, past grazing cattle and a few nimble-footed elk, an eagle circled briefly overhead. Above the yellowing grass and some pinkish red weed Holly couldn't name, green-gold chamisa lifted its autumn blooms in brushy clumps.

An hour or so into their ride, they came to a padlocked gate that separated Honeycomb Ranch from the public lands of the San Juan National Forest. Opening it from the saddle with a key that she'd remembered to thrust into her pocket, Holly waved her companions through, and shut it behind the three of them. After that, their climb grew steeper. However, it wasn't long before they reached the meadow she had in mind. From it, a vista of snowcapped peaks opened up. There was a broad outcropping of rock they could use as a picnic table.

"I'm hungry," Jake announced as they tied their horses to several saplings, giving them ample rope to graze. "Let's eat."

"Me, too!" Lisa chimed in.

Holly smiled as she unsnapped the leather bindings that held her blanket roll in place. "So what's new?" she teased, striding over to their dining spot and spreading the blanket so he and her stepdaughter could unload their meal. "You two are always starved, no matter how much I feed you!"

The "you two" and "always" of her statement implied a unity and depth in their relationship that was almost familial, she reflected as they dug into the food. Yet Jake had been part of their lives for just a few weeks. A drifter, he couldn't be counted on to stick around for long. Was she making a big mistake by letting him penetrate their circle of two that way—setting herself, and worse still, Lisa, up for a disappointment?

That the girl had grown inordinately fond of him, she had little doubt. Watching the two of them together only confirmed it. As they munched their sandwiches and demolished generous portions of the applesauce-raisin cake Holly had baked, Lisa listened avidly to Jake's story of a picnic in the woods with a part-Indian companion who'd worked for his mother when he was about her age. According to him, he and his mentor had gathered and trapped their food and cooked it over an open fire. They'd also spent the night in the woods.

Though Holly judged the story to be a tall tale, Lisa hung on every word. "Will you teach me to trap for my dinner, the way Johnney Red Deer taught you, in case I'm ever lost in the woods?" she begged, caught up in the romance of his adventure.

His mouth curved slightly. "If you insist. Sure you want to skin and cook a squirrel? Or a chipmunk?"

Realizing what was at stake, Lisa made a face.

"I think she's changed her mind," Holly suggested.

When at last they were finished, Holly and Jake put away the leftover food and stretched out on the blanket to gaze at the distant mountains while Lisa gathered a bouquet of the wildflowers that grew among the meadow's yellowing grass and weeds. At Holly's prompting to share a little more of his past, Jake told a few stories from his rodeo days. He admitted to having met Clint on one occasion.

"Tall, redheaded guy, as I remember," he said.

She nodded, trying to imagine the two of them together.

"He was one of the best," Jake added. "Somewhat older than me. I looked up to him."

When she asked how long he'd been in rodeo, he equivocated. "Too long," he responded, rolling over on his side to gaze into her eyes. "I decided to get out while I was in one piece."

She had to bite her tongue to keep from telling him he was still in pretty good shape.

Lisa saved her from herself by insisting they play a game of tag. Designating herself as "it," and the slab of rock they'd picnicked on as "home base," she closed her eyes and counted to twenty while Jake and Holly scattered. The high-spirited free-for-all that followed had them screaming with hilarity, particularly when Lisa managed to tag Jake and he caught Holly in the next breath. Holly ended up on the ground with Jake and Lisa piled on top of her.

Fully invested in the spirit of the game, Lisa jumped up screaming, "Holly...you're it!" and ran away as fast as her legs would carry her.

Jake didn't move. His breath warm and seductive against Holly's ear, the weight of his upper body crushing her breasts, he lay there looking at her. One of his denim-clad knees rested between her thighs. She could feel his manhood stiffen, the secret gateway to her womanhood quiver in anticipation as he pressed against her.

God, but she's beautiful, Jake thought as he smoothed a loose strand of hair back from her forehead. So honest and natural—sweet as honey in the comb. I could die of wanting her. On fire to kiss her, he started to lower his mouth to hers.

The moment coincided with Lisa's discovery that they hadn't moved. "C'mon, you guys," she yelled in exasperation, returning to tug at them. "You're not supposed to wrestle. Holly, it's your job to *chase* us!"

Her cheeks flushed, Holly wriggled to an upright position and did her best to comply with Lisa's instructions. Both relieved and wistful that she and Jake had been interrupted before they could kiss, she was careful not to look too directly at him. Within minutes, she was calling a halt to the game. A mass of clouds had rolled in from the west, threatening rain as they transformed the day from bright to gloomy.

Nobody said much as they saddled up and headed back to Honeycomb. Even Lisa looked thoughtful. Hoping the girl was tired rather than upset by what had nearly turned out to be an embarrassing episode, Holly decided nothing of the sort could be allowed to happen again. She'd have to speak to Jake. If he couldn't keep his distance, he'd have to look elsewhere for employment.

When they reached the barn, she offered to help Lisa carry the picnic things into the house while he saw to the horses, then asked the girl to put the food away by herself as they entered the kitchen. "I've got to run outside and check on something, okay?" she said.

Jake heard her approach from Comet's stall, where he was rubbing the filly down and currying her. Was Holly on her way to read him the riot act? Or did she want precisely what he wanted?

His employer's classic, unadorned features were a study in mixed emotions when she appeared. "I need to talk to you," she asserted, standing closer to him than prudence might have dictated.

Jake put down the currycomb and towel he was using with a deliberate gesture. "I don't see why," he answered, "when words won't solve the problem."

A moment later, his mouth was consuming hers.

Chapter Four

An explosion of fireworks illuminating the dim and dusty stall, Jake's kiss carried Holly beyond protest. All thought of ordering him to keep his distance fled. Instead of just dreaming about the possibility, she was in his arms. Demanding but gentle, his hands explored her body through the slender barrier of her clothing. Exacting a similar privilege, she held him close.

He smelled wonderful, like saddle leather and straw, the piny tang of cool mountain air against heated skin mingled with the expensive-smelling after-shave she liked so much. She wanted to drink him in. Savor him like the finest brandy. With all that she had and all that she was, she wanted to breathe his every breath.

She didn't retreat when his tongue teased her lips apart in imitation of the deeper communion he so obviously wanted. Or cavil at his flagrant seeking. Half-delirious with pleasure, she caressed the corded muscles of his back and shoulders. Though it had never happened that way with anyone, she was damp inside her jeans with wanting him.

Comet's soft blowing as she nuzzled the incomprehensible humans who were wrestling in her stall brought Holly to her senses. You can't do this, she ordered herself in panic, appalled at the ease with which she'd tumbled from her lofty defenses. Jake is a stranger. Your hired hand. You have responsibilities. This doesn't *mean* anything to him.

With Holly nestled in his arms, Jake was storming heaven's gate. What a wonder she is! he exulted, half-drunk with the privilege of caressing her. So ladylike and sweet, yet passionate as a lioness. A month of Sundays in her bed wouldn't be enough. A rover where women were concerned up to that point, he realized to his delight and consternation that he'd never be sated with her crushed-berry lips, the trim but rounded shape of her buttocks. Compelled by everything that was male and randy in him, he longed to sweep her beyond reason. Together, they'd mount the footholds to paradise.

Thoughts of forever were knocking at the threshold of his consciousness as he drew back sufficiently to rain little kisses on her face and neck. "Holly... Holly... can you possibly know what you do to me?" he whispered.

I know what you do to *me*, she thought. You cut me loose from every mooring of sanity and prudence. It has to stop! Pushing hard, with her palms splayed against his chest, she managed to extricate herself from his embrace.

"Probably not," she answered as he stared at her in surprise. "I'd rather you didn't share the gory details. What happened just now was as much my fault as yours. But it can't be repeated... not even to the limited extent that it occurred up on the mountain this afternoon. I have a ten-year-old stepdaughter to think about."

Astonished, Jake didn't answer her.

"I came back out here to tell you that," she persisted. "I want your word that, in the future, you'll keep your hands to yourself."

Tight-lipped and still hot with desire, Jake regarded her with narrowed eyes. If she kicked me off the ranch, it would serve me right, he acknowledged—not for kissing her, but for the deception I'm practicing. Perverse as always, he vowed not to let that happen if he could help it. With Holly, he'd discovered something that, previously, he'd only dreamed about.

"You're the boss," he said at last in a quiet voice. "You call the shots."

Her victory a hollow one when it came to the heart, Holly turned and strode back to the house. A short time later, his truck hurtled up the driveway in a cloud of dust. With a sinking feeling in the pit of her stomach, she wondered if he'd cleared out for good. Pride laced with fear kept her from checking his trailer to see if her guess was accurate.

When he didn't return by breakfast, she decided they wouldn't see him again. At once the life she'd made for herself and Lisa seemed dingier—a soul-empty place.

When Lisa asked where he was, she received a terse answer. "Sunday is Jake's day off," she informed the girl in a tone that didn't invite dialogue. "What he does with it is none of our affair."

After two thoroughly wretched nights spent tossing and turning in her bed, Holly wanted to fling her arms around Jake's neck when, on Monday morning, he showed up at the breakfast table. Reason kept her from going for it. Though Lisa gabbed his head off and hung on his every sentence, she and Jake barely exchanged two words. They remained uncommunicative with each other as they returned to the fencing project a short time later. Everything about his carriage and deportment suggested he wouldn't try to kiss her again. Ironically, her yearning for him only strengthened.

That week, as they raced to finish their work before the first heavy snowfall, they prepared to attend the dance. Having brought nothing but work clothes when he set out on his leave of absence, Jake settled for the best shirt and jeans of the lot. Holly made Lisa a red velveteen dress with a lace collar. She took in a flowered challis one with long sleeves and piqué ruching she'd worn when Clint was courting her. Thanks to all the exercise she'd gotten during the past several years, running the ranch without much help, it was too big for her.

At last, Saturday rolled around. The red disk of the sun was slipping behind the mountains, leaving a slowly fading swath of magenta-tinged clouds as, bathed, brushed and dressed in their best clothes beneath winter-weight parkas, Holly, Jake and Lisa assembled beside Holly's truck. Like lovers who recently have quarreled, Holly and Jake sought each other's eyes, then glanced away.

It had been like that all week. Meanwhile, they were late getting started. "Want to drive?" Holly asked, her breath pluming on the frosty air as she held out her keys.

Jake's shrug was nonchalant. "If you want."

Watching them, Lisa was clearly aware they weren't on the best of terms. Yet their estrangement didn't seem to bother her. Scrambling into the middle position in the truck's cab so that she acted as a physical buffer between them, she chattered enthusiastically about the evening ahead.

The huge Cunningham ranch, one of the more prosperous in the valley, was a thirty-minute drive from Honeycomb. By the time they reached it, a sea of trucks and four-wheel-drive vehicles surrounded its corral. Atop tall poles, the yard lights were blazing. A scarecrow made of straw and a huge pile of pumpkins had been set up beside the half-open barn door, which was festooned with welcome streamers in an array of fall colors. The sounds of fiddling, square-dance calls and bursts of laughter greeted them.

Inside, the festivities were already in full swing, lit by the cheerful glow of electrified lanterns that had been strung from the barn's rafters and along the edge of the hayloft. Pausing briefly to ask Holly's permission, Lisa quickly ran off to join several of her schoolmates, including her best friend, Jane Tørnquist. The granddaughter of Holly's closest neighbors, Emma and Lars Tørnquist, Jane was spending the school year in Larisson Valley while her parents were on temporary work assignment in Saudi Arabia.

Though she was happy to see Lisa enjoy herself, Holly couldn't help feeling self-conscious about arriving with her attractive hired hand in tow. It was almost as if they were dating. Painfully aware his presence might set tongues to wagging, she made a beeline for the Tørnquists, who were sipping cider from paper cups and chatting with some other neighbors as they watched the dancers. At least she could count on them to understand.

"Lars, Emma... Tom and Sandy... I'd like you to meet Jake McKenzie, who's been helping me fence the north pasture," she said, coloring slightly at the friendly but curious way they and the Tibbetts, the couple who ranched the property just south of hers, looked him up and down as they greeted him.

"Happy to meet you, Jake," Lars responded, his Scandinavian accent pronounced and his eyes twinkling behind wire-rimmed glasses as he pumped Jake's hand. "Holly's one of our favorite people, and she's long been in need of reliable help. I hope you plan to stay awhile."

"Any friend of Holly's is a friend of ours," Emma added.

A bit more reserved, the Tibbetts took turns shaking hands with him.

Returning everyone's hello with his usual firm grip and wry flash of smile, Jake didn't volunteer any more information about himself than absolutely necessary.

"I hear you helped Holly fix the barn roof," Tom Tibbetts commented.

Jake nodded. "It was our first project."

The men had been talking about the price of beef and government subsidies. After briefly questioning Jake about where he was from and probing his credentials as a ranch hand, they resumed their discussion of the topic. Sandy Tibbetts excused herself to speak with some friends. Taking up the slack, Emma recounted an anecdote involving Jane and some kittens that had taken up residence in the Tørnquist barn.

Her hand inadvertently brushing Jake's as she listened to Emma's story, Holly stole a quick glance at him.

Wanna dance? his blue eyes inquired. *Or will our practice in the kitchen go to waste?*

Nothing would have pleased her more than to take a turn on the dance floor with him. Unfortunately, she didn't trust herself to follow where it might lead. Their firestorm of a kiss a week earlier had taught her just how fragile her self-control *was* where he was concerned. She was also afraid of the gossip it might generate.

When she didn't encourage him with either word or look, he volunteered to get them some cider.

"Thanks, that'd be nice," Holly answered, regretting her qualms the moment he strode away from them, long and lean in his faded jeans and worn cowboy boots.

As soon as he was out of earshot, Emma moved closer. "So *that's* your new hand," her motherly neighbor said in an approving tone, gazing after him. "Lisa has described him to us. She said he was smart and fun...a very hard worker. But she didn't tell us how handsome he was!"

In Holly's estimation, Jake was the sexiest man on the planet. Old clothes and the occasional stubble of beard he sported only emphasized his looks by contrast. Yet she shrank from agreeing with Emma's appraisal. The proprietary thrill she felt at the praise her neighbor had lavished on him only added to her ambivalence.

"For the record, he sleeps in the old trailer next to the barn," she responded a trifle defensively. "Our arrangement is strictly business. He needed a job. And I needed help. It was that simple. There isn't any gossip circulating about us, I hope."

The corners of her mouth curving, as if she thought Holly protested too much, Emma gave her arm a reassuring pat. "Not to my knowledge," she said. "People around here know you too well to think you'd do anything scandalous. It's just that seeing you with a good-looking man the right age for you makes me realize how young and pretty you are...and how long it's been since you lost Clint. To my way of thinking, it's time there was a man in your life again."

Surely you're not suggesting I take up with an itinerant laborer, Holly wanted to retort, and then hated herself for thinking such disparaging thoughts. She glanced up as a respectable, fortysomething widower from Stony Creek approached and asked her to join him in a lively square-dance number. Eager to put paid to her conversation with Emma and prove to the world at large that she was a free agent, she quickly accepted.

Thus it happened that, when Jake returned with cups of ice-cold cider for them, she was dancing. From what he could tell, she appeared to be enjoying herself. Scowling, he set her cup aside. Though he did his best to evince a polite interest in Emma Tørnquist's murmured commentary as he sipped at his own beverage, his eyes didn't leave Holly's face.

Finally the widower returned her to her friends. He'd promised to call the next number. Not pausing to ask permission, Jake put down his cup and tucked his hand possessively through her arm.

"My turn," he insisted. "If you're thinking of refusing me, don't . . . unless you want to start a fuss."

Convinced everyone in the Cunninghams' oversize hay barn must be staring at them, Holly complied with his ultimatum. She was unsmiling, a little stiff, as they took their places in one of the circles that was forming. Once the fiddling started and her erstwhile partner began calling out the moves, however, she couldn't maintain her standoffish air. The music was too infectious, the feel of Jake's fingers gripping her waist through the fabric of her dress too welcome. She quickly learned that his skill as a dancer far surpassed his claims. Before long, they were exchanging amused, friendly glances as they strove to heed the caller's somewhat mixed-up instructions.

Things got exponentially a lot more serious when the widower from Stony Creek introduced a set of slower, ballroom-style numbers and they nestled more closely in each other's arms. For Holly, it was like kissing Jake in Comet's stall all over again, though their lips didn't meet. As if they'd been created for just that purpose, their hips moved in unison. Aching for the contact, their thighs brushed wantonly together.

It's as if we could make love right here in the Cunninghams' hay barn with my friends and neighbors looking on, yet not be impeded in our fulfillment, Holly thought, her heart pounding like a wild thing in her breast as she shut her eyes and pressed her cheek to his. *I should pull back. Conduct myself with greater decorum. Yet that's not what I want to do.* With everything that was womanly and willful in her, she longed to blend and merge with her tall partner until every trace of the individual boundaries that separated them had ceased to exist.

For Jake, her sudden softening, her melting into him, was more than his self-control could abrogate. Tugging her closer as his body responded with a passionate rush he couldn't quell, he let his thoughts fly past the deception that had brought him to her doorstep and dared to fantasize some kind of solution for them. To her, he knew, he was a mendicant cowboy, down on his luck and not necessarily to be trusted. *If he could talk her into forgiving him once she knew the truth, maybe there was hope for them.*

By the end of the set, he was temporarily indisposed. Resting one hand casually on her shoulder, he positioned Holly in front of him so that she screened his recovery while the crowd applauded the musicians, who'd been drawn from the local population. Fully cognizant of what he was doing and none too eager to share her knowledge with the world, Holly cooperated, her face a study in ambivalence.

Another round of lively square-dance numbers was about to start. "Do you want to dance again?" Jake asked, aware her former partner had completed his stint on stage and was headed in their direction.

Her defenses in a shambles thanks to the intimacy of their turn on the dance floor, Holly couldn't muster the fortitude to reject him. If people wanted to gossip, she'd let them. On the other hand, she couldn't abandon her most cherished principles. Unless she wanted to end up in bed with Jake, sans marriage, or—God help her—agree to tie the knot without careful consideration of what that would mean, she needed to cool things herself.

"Maybe we'd better sit this one out," she suggested.

I hope that means you won't be dancing with your admirer, either, Jake responded silently. Glancing about for Lisa, he spotted the girl wistfully tapping her toe on the far side of the dance floor. Clearly, she was yearning to participate. It didn't look as if she stood much chance. True to form, most of the boys her age were wrestling and talking among themselves—giving their female classmates a wide berth.

Jake couldn't help thinking of the way Clint had danced with his daughter shortly before his death, and wondering if the girl was remembering it, too. He turned back to Holly. "Mind if I ask Lisa, then?"

Surprise and gratitude lit her face. "Jake...*would* you?"

"I'd be happy to," he said.

Walking her back to where the Tørnquists continued to watch the dancers, Jake crossed the barn and made Lisa a little bow. Holly looked on as surprise and pleasure washed over her stepdaughter's face. Their heights as dissimilar as the contrasting colors of their hair, the shabbily dressed but dashing man and skinny redheaded schoolgirl took their places.

The first real snow of the year was falling an hour and a half later as, zipped into their parkas and toasty warm in the heated cab of Holly's truck, they drove back to Honeycomb with Lisa wedged between their bodies. Though at first the girl couldn't seem to stop talking about the evening's events, particularly the envy and excitement of her girlfriends when Jake had danced with her, it wasn't long before her lashes were fluttering lower and she was resting her head on Holly's shoulder. A country-western ballad was playing on the radio and, with a quiet glance at Holly, Jake turned down the volume.

How I wish things were different, Holly thought, enjoying the luxury of letting him care for them. Though none of us are related by blood, and I'm Jake's employer, not his lover, it's as if the three of us are in the process of becoming a family. If I shut my eyes and let my imagination carry me away, I can almost picture us kissing Lisa good-night and retiring to my room, snuggling cozy and secret beneath my down coverlet.

Envisioning them married and making a life together was jumping the gun, of course. She didn't know anything about Jake you couldn't discover by working side by side with a man for almost a month. And he hadn't volunteered much. I'd give anything if he were a local rancher . . . someone I'd known and trusted for several years, she thought, instead of a hired hand with a questionable past who turned up penniless on my doorstep. If the former were true, he could court me and rumors wouldn't fly. Everyone in the valley would know and approve of him.

For his part, though he felt the pleasure of their growing bond as keenly as she did, Jake was busy wishing he'd met Holly some other way—*any* way but the one he'd so brilliantly engineered. The fact was, she was beginning to mean a great deal to him. And his goose would be cooked with her the minute she learned whom he represented.

Damn it, he thought, trying not to grit his teeth in his frustration. I owe Dutch loyalty. . . both as his friend and as his attorney. And I genuinely support his right to interact with his granddaughter before she's all grown up. But I shouldn't have to throw away the best thing that's ever happened to me for his sake. There ought to be a way I can do right by him without spoiling my chances and torpedoing what Holly and Lisa have built together.

Unfortunately, he couldn't think of one that wouldn't leave him out in the cold. The possibility that Holly might end up there, too, with Dutch persuading a judge his blood tie to the girl ought to take precedence over the stepparent relationship she'd so lovingly nurtured, had begun to haunt him.

Too soon, from his point of view, they arrived at Honeycomb. Though the lights in the truck's cab came on when they opened the doors, letting in a blast of cold air, Lisa didn't fully wake. Lifting and carrying her into the house, Jake hung around in the kitchen while Holly helped the drowsy girl undress and tucked her into bed. When she reappeared, he got to his feet, hat in hand, to wish her a subdued good-night.

"The dance was fun—thanks for inviting me," he said.

Silent a moment, she gazed up at him. Had she missed something? He sounded so somber—almost as if he were bidding her goodbye. "I had fun, too," she answered at last. "Don't mention it."

I don't know what to do, Jake agonized a minute later, his head down and his boots leaving a distinctive trail of footprints in the snow as he made his way to his cramped and chilly trailer. I can't keep working beside her every day and not kiss her, hold her, want to make love to her. Yet she'll kick me off Honeycomb for good if I tell her the truth.

The following Saturday would be Halloween. Midday temperatures that had hovered in the mid-forties dropped to the low thirties and snow fell with increasing frequency as Holly and Jake struggled, beginning Monday, to finish the fencing project they'd inaugurated in more clement weather. Meanwhile, Jake's trailer, with its drafty seams and inadequate space heater, was freezing. After spending several nights fully dressed, shivering in his sleeping bag beneath several layers of blankets, he asked in desperation if he could camp on the kitchen floor, beside the fireplace.

Unable to refuse what she considered a reasonable request, Holly agreed with mixed emotions. It didn't surprise her that letting him sleep under her roof only made her longing for him more intense. She tried to sublimate it by planning and working on Lisa's Halloween costume, a Native American squaw outfit—to little effect.

Their proximity had a equally devastating effect on Jake. As they pounded fence posts and strung wire bundled to the nines, or hauled hay in the truck to outlying pastures for the stock, he longed to kiss her ruddy, increasingly chapped cheeks and shelter her from the frigid north wind inside his coat. Lacking any outlet for his passionate, protective urges, he began to find his attraction to her something of a torment. Worry over their inevitable clash when he told her the truth, coupled with a nagging sense of guilt over his failure to inform Dutch of his granddaughter's whereabouts, were having him for breakfast.

Though it seemed like months had elapsed instead of days, finally the week was over. Quitting time on Friday found Holly waiting behind the wheel of her truck in swirling snow as Jake got out and opened the barn door for her. A moment later, she was driving inside and turning off the engine.

He's got the manners of a diplomat and the physique of a cowboy, she thought, helplessly drawn to him as he held open the cab door for her. He didn't step aside and, perforce, they were standing very close.

It was now or never. "I suppose you heard—the Tørnquists are holding a Halloween party for Jane and her girlfriends from school at their house tomorrow night," she announced tentatively. "Since there are miles between

neighbors in the valley and kids can't trick-or-treat from
door to door..."

Jake tilted his head slightly to one side as he regarded her.
Was she advertising the fact that she'd be home alone all
evening? Somehow he doubted it. "Lisa mentioned it once
or twice," he said.

"Well, umm..." She paused. "Lars has a lodge meeting
in Pagosa Springs tomorrow afternoon. He'll be back late.
Emma was wondering if we could come over to help. You
don't have to go, if you don't want. It isn't a requirement of
your job or anything. Of course you know Lisa would love
it if you did."

Her ambivalence was painfully clear to him. What about
you? he countered silently. Would *you* love it? "I was
thinking of driving into Pagosa Springs myself tomorrow
evening for a little R and R," he said indifferently. "But it's
nothing I can't cancel. I don't mind driving over with you
if you think I could be of help."

Though Jake's backhanded acceptance of her invitation
drove a speculative stake of jealousy through Holly's heart,
the evening turned out well. A somewhat incongruous sight
with her springy red curls as Sacajawea, guide to Lewis and
Clark, Lisa won a prize for the most authentic costume and
aced the apple-bobbing contest. Jake was in demand—in
part because several of her friends remembered him as the
man who'd asked her to dance at the Cunninghams' party.
But it was his unsuspected talent for telling ghost stories that
won him the most points with Lisa's classmates.

"Know what?" Emma whispered to Holly as they set out
mugs for hot chocolate and a huge tray of homemade
doughnuts. "Your Jake would make a good father. He's got
Jane and Lisa and all their friends eating out of his hand."

Forced to agree, provided he was capable of commitment, Holly wasn't about to admit it to her well-meaning

neighbor. "Emma, please!" she protested, twin spots of color flooding her cheeks. "He's not *my* Jake...simply my employee. I don't even expect the situation to be permanent."

As if he'd planned it that way on purpose, Lars returned home from his meeting as the doughnuts and hot chocolate were being served. "I see I arrived at the proper moment," he joked, winking at Jane's friends and giving his wife a pacifying kiss on the cheek. "Good to see you, Holly... Jake. You got that fencing finished yet? Let me know if you need any help."

With Lars ensconced in his favorite easy chair, everyone settled down to munch and sip and listen to a final tale of the supernatural delivered by Jake in deliciously sepulchral tones. When at last it was over, and parents began arriving to pick up their daughters, Jane and Lisa put their heads together. A moment later, Lisa was begging for permission to spend the night.

"Jane can lend me a pair of pajamas and a robe," she cajoled earnestly. "Pretty please with sugar on it, Holly...say yes!"

Jane was tugging at her grandfather's hand. "Tell Mrs. Yarborough it's okay...that Lisa won't be any trouble," she begged.

Smiling as he filled his pipe, Lars took his time about answering. "It would be our pleasure to have Lisa as our guest," he affirmed at last in his courtly, old-world way. "Tomorrow's Sunday. I'll bring her home first thing in the morning, Holly, so you won't have to come after her."

A quick glance at Emma revealed that the spontaneous arrangements were fine with her. Somewhat reluctantly, because giving them her stamp of approval meant she and Jake would sleep under the same roof without the mediating influence of Lisa's presence, Holly gave in.

"Looks like you've got me outnumbered," she told her stepdaughter with an indulgent shake of her head. "You can stay...provided you promise to get some sleep and don't keep Mr. Tørnquist waiting tomorrow when he's ready to bring you home. Don't forget...you have chores to do that got shunted aside while you were talking on the phone to Jane and putting on your Indian makeup this afternoon."

Without Lisa's chatter to provide a distraction, the drive back to Honeycomb was quiet in the extreme. Tonight, Holly thought with a little shiver that was more excitement than cold, there'll be no ten-year-old to tuck into bed. Jake won't go trudging off to his trailer. We'll sleep alone under the same roof—with just a wall separating us.

Parking the truck inside the barn where it would be more likely to start in the morning if the temperature dropped, they headed toward the porch. A single lamp had been left burning in the living room. Unlocking the front door, Holly preceded Jake inside. Her keen awareness of the quandary their relationship had become sharpened perceptibly when he didn't wish her a routine good-night or move to fetch his sleeping bag from behind the couch. The charged quality of the atmosphere between them all but forced her to say something.

"Would you like a cup of coffee to chase away the chill?" she asked, pulling off her boots as she attempted to keep the unsteadiness she felt from surfacing in her voice. "I have some decaf that won't keep us awake...."

In the play of shadow and light that revealed the room's familiar furnishings, Jake's eyes had taken on their smoky look. "Wanting you keeps me awake," he answered.

A moment later, they were in each other's arms.

Chapter Five

During their absence at the Tørnquists' party, the carefully banked blaze in Holly's fireplace had almost gone out. She kept her bottled-gas furnace set at sixty-five degrees to save on fuel bills. Yet she and Jake didn't feel the chill that was gathering in her living room. After so much yearning, they were making their own heat.

Bold but subtly questioning, his tongue parted her lips. A little sigh signaled her willingness to continue as she slipped her arms about his neck. Like it or not, this cowboy with a dubious past was the man for her. They were alone in the house, hidden from prying eyes. In that sequestered, unfettered moment, second-guessing her heart's desire wasn't on her agenda.

Running his hands down the slender curves of her body the way he'd wanted to do since the moment he'd set eyes on her, Jake was dumbfounded by her cooperation. Was the wholesome blond rancher who'd seemed so out of reach really kissing him back like a house afire? Or was he simply dreaming it? God knew, since their ill-fated skirmish in Comet's stall, he'd pictured it happening often enough.

He couldn't ignore the possibility that he was courting danger. With each fresh liberty he took, he might goad her further than she was willing to go. Prodding her past the point where she'd slap his face and order him off her property was the last thing he wanted. He had to take the risk. Faint heart never won a thing that mattered to you, he thought with a twinge of fatalism, slipping his hands beneath her sweater to claim her breasts.

Holly's gasp of delight was smothered against his mouth. Erect beneath the stretch-lace fabric of her bra, her nipples telegraphed inflammatory messages to her deepest places. Helpless to withstand them, she let wave after wave of sensation wash over her.

Passion was a river overflowing its banks and she was a leaf on its current. With all the generosity that had gone begging until he'd appeared at her gate, she longed to connect with Jake in every way possible, make her tall, bewitching ranch hand an unconditional present of who she was.

She surprised them both by pulling her sweater over her head. A moment later, she was unhooking her bra's front clasp and sliding its straps down her arms.

Jake's breath caught in his throat to see Holly revealed that way. His arousal intensified. Pliant, exquisite, too perfect for a man who hadn't always been selective in his choices, she stood naked to the waist in a nimbus of lamplight—a virgin in spirit, he guessed, despite her widowhood, whereas he'd known too many women without learning anything of substance from them.

With her, he'd immerse himself in life's mysteries, cede his carefully guarded separateness. Aware at some subliminal level that loving and winning her could heal the malaise that had afflicted him, he responded by taking off his shirt and positioning her against his chest.

So sweetly calculated to inflame her ardor, the gesture blew her away. Operating solely on instinct, she insinuated herself against him. In such proximity, his readiness to make love to her wasn't any secret.

Gray eyes blurring into blue, they kissed. Nipple seduced nipple. Half out of his head, Jake tugged her closer. He was trembling with his need for her.

Would she let him make love to her? Too hot not to pursue an answer, he dared to unzip her jeans. When she didn't object, he dragged them down her hips, raining blunt, adoring kisses on her neck as he helped her step free of them. Her cotton bikini panties came next, to be discarded with her socks in a little heap.

Pale as the dusting of snow that lay on Honeycomb Ranch in contrast to the outdoor tan that lingered on her face and arms, the smooth curve of Holly's buttocks was his to caress. Her nest of coarse, Scandinavian-blond curls awaited his fingertips.

To Holly, the corded muscles of Jake's biceps and the erect manhood that pressed against the front of his jeans were nothing short of breathtaking. She ached to bury her face against the tangled mat of crisp, dark chest hair that plunged toward his belt in a narrowing seam, draw down his zipper and learn his shape with her fingertips.

It would be their first time together. Despite a storm of longing that cried for immediate gratification, Jake wanted it to be special. Lifting Holly in his arms, he bypassed the couch and carried her into her bedroom.

They didn't switch on a light. Like frost, like opals, moonlight spilled across her down coverlet, barely illuminating the honeyed wood tones of her log walls and beamed ceiling. Their eyes gleamed black in the shadows it didn't penetrate as they gazed at each other.

Drowning in awe, Jake held Holly close. He was on fire with wanting her. "Tell me what you want," he whispered.

Everything you have, her heart clamored. *Nothing less will be enough.*

Flickering to the bed in anticipation of what they'd do, her gaze was caught and held by a throw pillow Lisa had painstakingly embroidered for her the previous Mother's Day. To The Best Holly In The World, it proclaimed mischievously in uneven block letters. Misgivings seized her, though she tried to quell them. The daughter Clint had placed in her care deserved better than the action she was contemplating.

"Jake...we can't make love," she whispered.

Was she making some kind of joke? If so, it wasn't funny. "Surely you're kidding," he said after a moment.

Turning her back on what they both wanted would be the hardest thing she'd ever had to do. To her regret, she didn't have any other choice. "I have a stepdaughter who trusts me to honor the principles I'm instilling in her," she tried to explain. "If I go against them behind her back I'll never forgive myself."

His thoughts in turmoil, he set her on her feet. "What am I supposed to say to that?" he asked. Aware his tone was harsh with disappointment, he quickly softened it. "Lisa's gone for the night," he added more reasonably. "She'd never have to know."

Though his willingness to deceive her stepdaughter hurt, Holly didn't hold it against him. What had transpired between them had been her doing as much as his. From a cowboy down on his luck who'd talked her into hiring him, Jake McKenzie had turned into the man she loved.

She hadn't previously admitted her feelings, even to herself. As the discovery sank in, she struggled to deal with the situation at hand. "Jake," she begged, adding as she felt him tense further, "please try to understand. I can't give myself to you the way you want…not because I don't want it, too, but because we aren't married. I don't believe in sex between unmarried people."

Was she saying she wanted to marry him? Somehow, Jake doubted it. She might crave him physically, even enjoy his company. But under the circumstances she'd never consider him husband material. In her eyes, he felt certain, he was nothing more than an itinerant ranch hand, here today and gone tomorrow. He wouldn't merit her trust.

What a fool I was to approach her under false colors, he thought. Yet he knew she wouldn't have let Dutch Hargrett's lawyer get within ten feet of her. "Do you mean to say," he asked softly, his passion fading, "that, after getting all worked up, we're just going to say good-night?"

Holly was on the verge of tears. There were names for women like her. *Tease* was one of them. Yet she'd never intended anything of the sort. "If you're willing, we could hold each other under the blankets," she proposed.

About to dismiss the notion out of hand and argue forcefully for what he wanted, Jake didn't want to cause a rift between them. He guessed that was just what would happen if he pressed his case. Against his will, he was forced to admire her strength of principle. Meanwhile, it was tellingly clear that her feelings mattered a great deal to him.

"Don't cry, darlin'," he soothed, wrapping his arms around her and gently stroking the satin skin of her back and shoulders. "For tonight, holding you will be enough."

Abjectly grateful, Holly nestled close.

The room was bone-chillingly cold. Yet Jake didn't want her in a nightgown. Before she could make a move to cover up, he tugged off his boots and kicked them aside, dropped his jeans and undershorts on the braided rug beside her bed.

Her eyes devouring his nakedness, Holly didn't protest. Since their return from the Tørnquists' party, a bridge had been crossed. Getting into bed and holding back the coverlet for him, she welcomed him into her embrace.

After so many weeks of pretending he was just an employee, she would sleep with Jake. Share her body heat with him. Inhale his skin-scent. Unlike the typical roving cowpoke she'd believed him to be, he hadn't stormed out, left Honeycomb for good when she'd refused to make love to him. *He'd stuck around.*

Her head pillowed on his shoulder, Holly knew what his forbearance had cost. The price had been equally compelling for her. What will happen tomorrow and the next day? she wondered as the first wisps of dreams loosened her hold on events. Will I be able to make my convictions stick? Meanwhile, Lisa would be back in the morning. Their every action would be chaperoned.

For his part, though the pleasure of cuddling Holly naked was deep, Jake's thoughts had returned to the basic quandary that was consuming him. I've got to set things straight with her, he vowed, clear the way for us to have a relationship.

The question was, how to do it. He knew without having to be told that, for Holly, the truth about who he was and who he represented would be abhorrent in the extreme. At minimum, she'd order him off the property. In all likelihood, she'd refuse to speak to him. It was anyone's guess whether, over time, her position would soften. Now that he knew her better, he feared it would prove unyielding.

Eight hours later, sunlight was streaming in the window. Emanating from a slight distance but getting closer, a noise disturbed the tranquility of Holly's room. Her eyelids fluttered open. Drowsily, she decided that it was coming from a pickup truck. From what she could tell, it was approaching the house.

Beside her, Jake was sleeping peacefully.

Lars! she realized, sitting bolt upright. He's returning Lisa as promised!

Hurling herself from the bed as if she'd been propelled by a slingshot, Holly tore into the living area. Her jeans, sweater and underwear lay on the floor in a wrinkled heap.

Not pausing to catch her breath, she dragged them on and scooped up Jake's sweater. "Here . . . get dressed!" she ordered him in panic, racing back into the bedroom and shaking him by the shoulders. "Lars is arriving with Lisa! We can't let them catch us like this!"

Blinking the sleep from his eyes, Jake complied as quickly as he could. He was in the kitchen, an overnight stubble of beard shadowing his jaw as he rebuilt the fire, when Lars rapped lightly and entered, assuming a welcome.

Jane and Lisa were with him. While Jake put on the coffee and tried to make intelligent conversation in his groggy state, Holly hung back in the bedroom, furiously brushing and rebraiding her unkempt hair. As quickly as possible, so that it would seem she'd been up for a while, she reentered the kitchen carrying a load of laundry in a wicker basket and bid her visitors a cheery hello.

Jake's sleeping bag wasn't in its usual place, but that was probably for the best. There wasn't any reason for Lars to suspect he'd slept with her. Its presence beside the hearth would only invite speculation. The way her stepdaughter was chattering away with Jane, she doubted the girl would sense anything was amiss.

To her consternation, she realized suddenly that Jake was barefoot. His boots were probably under her bed! Clearly he hadn't walked to the house from his trailer that way. If he noticed, Lars would realize they were sleeping under the same roof.

So far, her neighbor seemed oblivious. Given enough time, though, he'd spot the inconsistency, she guessed. So would Lisa, the moment Jane left, or Jake had to perform some outdoor task. He could hardly fetch his missing footgear from her bedroom.

To Holly's relief, neither scenario materialized. Finishing his coffee, Lars announced it was time to go. He parried the girls' usual request for more time together with his customary good nature.

"Jane has some cleanup tasks to perform before we can drive to Pagosa Springs to spend Sunday with relatives," he explained with a smile. "You know, Lisa, you and Jane will see each other again in less than twenty-four hours, on the school bus."

That made it roughly twenty-four hours until she and Jake were alone again at Honeycomb. What would happen then? Murmuring something about having forgotten to strip her bed, Holly removed Jake's boots from her room under cover of a pile of sheets. She managed to slip them to him as Lisa was waving goodbye to her friend.

The close call had Holly rethinking her behavior. If she hadn't awakened at the sound of Lars's truck, Lisa would almost certainly have discovered them in bed together. Despite the fact that nothing had happened, she'd been wrong to sleep with Jake.

When he tried to kiss her by the barn later that morning, she sidestepped his embrace.

"What's wrong?" he asked, though her rejection didn't surprise him much.

Holly had difficulty meeting his eyes. Somehow she managed it. "I enjoyed what we ended up doing last night... as much as you seemed to," she confessed awkwardly. "But I don't think we should do it again. If we hadn't awakened in time, Lisa would have caught us. I'm a parent in addition to being a woman with desires and urges. I won't conduct an affair in the house where my stepdaughter's growing up. Lisa's real mother was a tramp. *I* plan to set a good example for her."

For what seemed an eternity, he didn't speak as he regarded her from beneath the brim of his cowboy hat. Then, "It's your call to make, Holly," he rejoined in a monotone.

Determined to have her as he watched her slim, somewhat melancholy figure retreat to the house, Jake decided he might as well drive into Larisson and phone Dutch. He'd been thoroughly negligent about calling in progress reports. Though he didn't intend to inform his friend and client that he'd located his missing granddaughter, the brief absence from Honeycomb would help clear his head.

Holly watched his truck head up the driveway with regret and foreboding. After what had happened, she couldn't blame Jake for seeking out a change of scene. She only hoped it wouldn't be permanent.

Jake quaffed a soft drink from a vending machine as he dialed Dutch's private number from a phone booth at Larisson's only gas station.

The older man's energy level soared perceptibly on hearing his voice. "Jake, my boy!" he cried. "I hope you're calling with good news. We have a room all decorated and waiting...."

Assailed with guilt over the double deception he was playing out, Jake was forced to betray Holly or lie to Dutch. He chose the latter course. "Take it easy, old friend," he said, applying the brakes to Dutch's enthusiasm as gently as he could. "I haven't found Lisa yet. But I've got a new lead...."

Never an easy man to thwart, Dutch staged one of his minor explosions. "Damn it!" he swore. "You've been gone for ages! When am I going to see some action?" There was a pause. "Don't tell me there's a woman mixed up in this...."

The irony of Dutch's wild guess was like a kick in the stomach for Jake. "Not in the way you're insinuating," he said hastily. Afraid the older man would put two and two together, he strove for an audible shrug. "It's been a while since we talked, that's all," he related. "I decided to check in, and—"

Impatient though he was to recover his granddaughter, Dutch had other worries. "Good thing you did," he interrupted. "I need you back in Durango...yesterday."

By now, Jake had begun to feel his real life was based in Larisson Valley with Holly and Lisa rather than in Durango, with his fancy new house and successful law firm. Uncertain how he was going to resolve the tangled mess his life had become, he quickly extracted the reason for Dutch's statement.

After a year of motions and bargaining, the Blackwell case—an important civil suit Jake had been handling prior to his departure—had suddenly reached the trial stage. Dutch had insisted one of his partners could handle it when that had suited his purposes. Now that push had come to shove, however, he wanted his most trusted counsel at the helm.

"Surely you can give up a few days of your leave as a favor to me," he wheedled.

Assessing the consequences of temporarily abandoning Holly at that juncture in their relationship, Jake tried to stall. "Can't it wait?" he backpedaled.

Dutch's answer was unequivocal. He planned to meet with the opposition in the morning in a last-ditch attempt to settle out of court. He wanted Jake there. "Where are you?" he asked.

Though Jake declined to name his exact location on the grounds that his sabbatical wouldn't be worth mud if it got out, he admitted to being a three-hour drive away.

"Terrific!" Dutch answered. "Bernie and I will expect you for supper. Try not to be late."

The evening meal at the Hargrett estate was served at 6:00 p.m. sharp. Jake answered that he'd do his best to make it. Returning the pay-phone receiver to its cradle, he reflected that resolving the Blackwell matter would take several days. He'd have to let Holly know he needed some personal time and hope she understood.

Returning to the ranch to inform her was out of the question. For one thing, it would take too long. But that wasn't his only reason. If they talked face-to-face, he might break down and tell her the truth.

He dialed her number with mixed emotions. After four rings, the answering tape came on. She and Lisa had probably gone outdoors. Anxious to depart so he could discharge his responsibilities to Dutch and return to them, he decided to leave a message.

"I, uh, have to go away for a few days on personal business," he mumbled by way of explanation. "Sorry if it interferes with the work. See you."

A chill gripped Holly an hour or so later as she listened to his cryptic message. Filled with regret over the way she'd handled their conversation by the barn that morning, she quickly put her own spin on the situation. Frustrated by her rejection, Jake had left to find himself another woman.

* * *

To Jake's chagrin, his informal meeting with Dutch's adversaries the next morning turned out to be a lost cause. The case would go to trial on Tuesday and last well into the next week, he guessed. He didn't have a prayer of convincing Dutch he didn't need to stick around and handle it.

As Holly fumed and wept, picturing him with a rival, Jake's trial proved the axiom that the wheels of justice turn slowly. Unable to explain his absence in a way that would make sense to her, he couldn't bring himself to call again.

She was suffering the torments of the damned by the time that, unknown to her, the trial entered its second week. Somehow, she managed to maintain an upbeat, unconcerned front for Lisa, who missed Jake and kept asking when he'd return.

Alone in her room each night after her stepdaughter had gone to bed, it was a different story. In her agonized recriminations, Jake played alternating roles. Sometimes she saw him as an innocent man whom she'd willfully misled. Then her mood would shift, and he'd become a bounder who'd mocked her virtue by seeking a less principled playmate.

By the time a second week had passed, she was positive they wouldn't see him again. She was at the height of her misery the second Saturday after his departure when Emma called. Her nearest neighbor was breezy but curious. Lisa had mentioned Jake's absence more than a week earlier. Had he returned yet?

Holly's toneless "No," told the tale in a nutshell.

Emma was silent a moment. "There's quite a bit of snow on the ground after last night," she observed. "But the roads are clear. Why don't you and Lisa come over for cherry pie? There's someone here I'd like you to meet."

A bit listlessly, Holly agreed for Lisa's sake.

The someone in question turned out to be the Tørn-quists' younger son, Nels, a single geologist about Holly's age who specialized in oil exploration. A younger, blonder version of Lars with Emma's thousand-watt smile, he was both friendly and courteous.

"Can you believe it?" He beamed as he, his parents, Holly and the girls consumed generous slices of Emma's pie at the latter's sunny kitchen table. "I'm off work for three whole weeks!"

"Tell them why," Lars prompted indulgently.

His gaze meeting Holly's, Nels explained that he'd be on location in Siberia for six to eight months. Because of the anticipated rigors of his assignment, his employer had granted him compensatory leave. Lacking anyone special in his life, he'd chosen to spend most of the time with his parents.

"For once, I'll be here on Thanksgiving to wrestle Jane for the wishbone," he said, giving his niece a wink. "Will you and Lisa be joining us, Holly?"

"Please do," Emma chimed in. "We'd love to have you."

If Jake doesn't return, Thanksgiving will be a world-class downer, Holly thought. Celebrating with the Tørnquists would make it bearable. "Thanks, we just might take you up on that," she said.

The visit with Emma, Nels, Lars and Jane was obviously great fun for Lisa and went a long way toward distracting Holly from what was bothering her. Though she was still depressed over Jake, she went along with Nels's suggestion that they drive into Larisson and see a movie while Jane and Lisa remained at home with his parents.

Meanwhile, in Durango, Jake had won his case. Announcing his verdict late Friday afternoon, the judge had found in favor of Dutch's company. Free to return to Honeycomb, Jake had decided to crash at his place north of town for the night. With the trial behind him, he'd needed some time to think.

Though he'd come to several conclusions—for instance, acknowledging the fact that he was serious about Holly and wanted to make a life with her—he hadn't been able to think of any way to tell her the truth about himself. His conflict-of-interest problem where Dutch was concerned was still a major obstacle. He couldn't stop worrying about Lisa's future. By now he was convinced that her primary place was with Holly, though he thought she ought to know her grandparents.

Driving a stretch of the partly snowpacked highway that led to Silverton in his sleek Mercedes early Saturday afternoon as a tension-relieving exercise hadn't helped much. In the absence of easy solutions now, he was packing a few things to return to the simpler life of Larisson Valley—a heavier coat, several more sweaters, a new toothbrush.

About to leave with them stashed in a beat-up suitcase from his post-Vietnam days, he hesitated and crossed the thickly carpeted floor of his bedroom to his concealed wall safe. Moving aside a framed oil painting of cowboys in the Tetons, he dialed the combination and retrieved what he wanted.

Pausing to gaze at the worn gold band set with a row of five small garnets that had once belonged to his mother, he slipped it into one of his billfold's inner pockets. The ghost of a smile tugged at the corners of his mouth. He might not get what he wanted. But his inner man knew what he was shooting for.

Moments later, whistling a popular country-western tune slightly off-key, he was in his beat-up red truck, starting the engine. Eagerness to see the two people who mattered most to him in the world lent impetus to his foot on the gas pedal as his old truck burned up the miles that separated them.

Buoyed by the hope that things would be all right, his spirits plummeted when he reached the ranch to find nobody home. Where were Holly and Lisa? Since the weather had gotten nippy, they'd usually spent their Sunday afternoons doing mother-daughter things like cutting out dress patterns and making cookies.

Letting himself in with the spare key he knew Holly kept wedged in a crevice between some logs at the back of the house, he went directly to the telephone. If anybody knew their whereabouts, it would be Emma Tørnquist.

Holly's motherly neighbor answered on the second ring. "Jake, where *are* you?" she exclaimed. "Back at Honeycomb? Yes, Lisa and Holly were here. As a matter of fact, Lisa still is. Holly went to a movie in Larisson with our son, Nels."

Jake was caught off guard. He hadn't realized there was a Nels Tørnquist. "Any idea what time they'll be back?" he asked, unable to keep the frown that drew his brows together from coloring his question.

If she caught a note of jealousy in his voice, Emma didn't remark on it. "Nels and Holly are coming in the door right now," she answered. "She and Lisa should be home in a little while."

Unaware of Jake's return, Holly let Lisa, Jane and Nels talk her into staying for homemade pizza, which was almost ready to come out of the oven. It was only later, after everyone had eaten their fill and she volunteered to help Emma clear the table that the latter had a private chance to talk with her.

"Your hired man's back," the older woman whispered with a smile.

Jolted from her despondency, Holly felt as if she'd received a mild electrical shock. *Jake,* she thought, yearning toward him with all her strength, though her trust was tarnished by doubt over what she'd convinced herself was his defection.

"What makes you think so?" she asked, not quite believing it. "He wasn't there when we left."

Emma gave her arm a reassuring pat. "He phoned just as you and Nels were coming up the driveway," she answered. "He sounded awfully anxious to see you."

If he's so anxious, Holly thought, why did he stay away so long? It crossed her mind that he might have come back for the remaining wages she owed him. If that's his only reason, she speculated, he won't stick around long.

When she told Lisa about Jake's return as they drove home, the girl was ecstatic. "Wow...cool!" she exclaimed. "I told you he'd come back, Holly. He *likes* living with us at Honeycomb."

A bundle of conflicting emotions as they turned off the county highway and headed up the driveway toward their house, Holly didn't answer. She wasn't sure she wanted to see Jake. How could she bear to look him in the eye—and imagine him with another woman?

He'd left his truck parked directly outside the front door instead of in its usual place behind the barn. Though the lapse argued for the eagerness Emma had attributed to him, Holly refused to see it that way. No doubt he's poised for a quick departure, she thought, wounding herself with the prospect.

The moment she brought the pickup to a stop, Lisa bounded out of the cab and ran like a champion sprinter for the house. Holly followed at a more decorous pace. Pausing to stamp the snow off her boots on the porch before entering her kitchen-and-living area, she was just in time to see her stepdaughter hugging Jake.

Freshly shaved, clad in faded jeans and a reindeer-patterned sweater she didn't remember seeing on him, he was all man and just as beautiful as she remembered. God, but she wanted him. The sad truth was that, whatever he'd done during his two weeks away from her, she loved him every bit as much.

She didn't plan to indulge her craving. Or to share her feelings with him.

The top of Lisa's head, with its exuberant mass of carroty curls escaping from a knitted cap, came to the midway point on Jake's chest. Her arms were twined about his waist the way she'd once wrapped them about Clint's. "I'm soooo glad you're back, Jake," she confessed, her feet all but dancing a jig of welcome as she continued to embrace him.

"Me, too, pumpkin."

The laugh lines beside Jake's mouth flashed deeper as he swept off the cap to ruffle Lisa's hair, then vanished as he met Holly's gaze. She was a sight for sore eyes, if not a sore heart. *What's your relationship with Nels Tørnquist?* he wanted to ask. *Is he the competition I have to face?*

Thanks to the way he'd gone off and left her without a decent explanation, he didn't have the right. "I'm back," he announced, stating the obvious. "Do I still have a job?"

A wave of relief broke over Holly, mixed with anger that he should continue to define their relationship that way. She shrugged. "I still need help," she answered with a take-it-or-leave-it expression, turning away to hang up her parka in the coat closet.

Chapter Six

At Lars and Emma's insistence, Holly, Lisa and Jake would have Thanksgiving dinner with them. Plagued by unresolved suspicions about what her dark-haired ranch hand had been doing during his two-week absence from Honeycomb, Holly was ambivalent about including him. Yet she didn't feel as if she had much choice. She could scarcely leave him at home on a day that epitomized good cheer and feasting to dine alone, on cold cuts. For one thing, Lisa wouldn't hear of it. And, for another, she cared about him too much.

Never one to lack information about a rival or the op-posing side in a lawsuit, Jake knew Nels would be present to vie for Holly's attention. Though he hadn't met the blond geologist, a man he'd probably like under any other cir-cumstances, he'd heard about him from Lisa.

He knew Nels would be leaving for Siberia in a week or so. Since the assignment wasn't permanent, the pending absence didn't set his mind at rest. As he sat beside the fire in Holly's cozy living room his first week back, helping Lisa with her math homework, he couldn't seem to stop imagining what might happen when Nels returned. Or keep from paying close attention to Holly's side of her phone conversation with him.

Finally, on a day of leaden skies and falling temperatures, he had his chance to evaluate Nels in person. Dressed in their best casual clothing, which for him was his reindeer sweater and freshly laundered jeans, they were seated across from each other at the Tørnquists' dining room table.

Between them lay a groaning board of sumptuous-looking food, including a perfectly basted turkey and roast venison with wild rice, plus all the trimmings, including homemade stuffing, scalloped corn, candied sweet potatoes and an array of Lars's favorite Swedish delicacies. On a nearby sideboard reposed the expertly made mince and pumpkin pies Holly had baked earlier that day while Jake had completed their daily chores, along with one of Emma's famous lingonberry tortes.

As grace was said and the meal got under way, Jake couldn't help noticing that most of the Tørnquist son's attention was focused on the slim, blond rancher he wanted for his own. Confining her answers to nods and monosyllables, she smiled noncommittally at Nels in the candlelight.

She seemed to have more to say to Emma, Lars, Lisa and Jane—even the Tørnquists' hired men, Hank Jeffries and Charlie Gutierrez—than she did to Jake. In truth, she barely glanced in his direction, though once or twice, when he least expected it, he caught her studying him.

When at last everyone was stuffed to the gills and conversation had begun to lag, Hank and Charlie excused themselves and went outside to tend the stock. Holly, Nels and Lars volunteered to clear the table and do up the dishes in order to give Emma a well-deserved rest. At a prodding glance from Holly, Lisa and Jane quickly offered to help.

"You can count on me, too," Jake said, starting to stack a pile of sticky dessert plates.

Emma forestalled him with a gentle touch. "Come...talk to me," she requested, leading him toward the living room and a pair of wingback chairs that stood on either side of the Tørnquists' massive stone fireplace. "If you don't, there won't be an inch of elbow room left in the kitchen. And I'll be bored to death."

As he parried Emma's seemingly offhand questions about his life prior to his arrival at Honeycomb, Jake strained to catch snatches of the lively conversation that was going on in the kitchen. He groaned silently when, once the dishes were finished, Holly and Nels emerged in search of their coats and boots.

"We're going to take an after-dinner walk," Nels explained.

Getting to his feet with every intention of accompanying them, Jake was promptly waylaid by Jane and Lisa, who had talked Lars into playing a card game called Push, and wanted a fourth at the table. With Lisa smiling up at him expectantly, he couldn't say no.

"Sounds like fun," he declared, deciding to make the best of the situation.

Assailed by a stiff north wind and snow as fine as soap powder, Holly and Nels didn't go far. At his suggestion, they paused on the lee side of the Tørnquists' massive barn beneath some evergreens.

"I wonder if it's this cold in Siberia," Nels said facetiously.

"Colder, I would think," Holly answered in all seriousness, bracing herself for some kind of declaration.

He didn't keep her waiting long. "As you know, I'm leaving tomorrow," he said. "I'll be gone for at least six months...maybe eight. That's quite a while and I was wondering if you'd write to me. As you've probably guessed, I'd like the chance to know you better when I return."

He was so nice, so uncomplicated. Unlike Jake, an open book. Before gazing into the latter's devastating blue eyes and hiring him to help out on her ranch, she'd probably have encouraged Nels. Now she couldn't. The change in outlook spoke volumes about her feelings.

He was waiting for an answer.

"Nels," she said gently, holding up a hand to stop him when it looked as if he'd interrupt, "I like you a lot. But I'm afraid exchanging letters would be pointless. I'm in love with someone else...a man I'll probably never marry."

Absorbing the rejection, Nels regarded her quietly for a moment. "It's Jake McKenzie, isn't it?" he said. "I saw the way he was looking at you during dinner. You do a better job of camouflaging your feelings than he does."

An experienced judge of human nature thanks to his years as a trial lawyer and business negotiator, Jake assessed the look on Nels's face when they returned to the house and breathed a sigh of relief. There was still hope for him.

His observation was to sustain him during his continued exile from Holly's confidence as Christmas approached. Meanwhile, it had begun to snow in earnest. In addition to her usual chores, Holly was up to her neck in Christmas preparations. From the moment she'd become Lisa's stepmother, she'd always tried to make the holidays special for the girl. This year, in addition to ordering her a Sony Walkman she could ill afford and baking eight varieties of cookies, she was secretly making Lisa a complete wardrobe for her cherished Barbie doll.

Each evening, when his day's work was done, Jake pitched in, warming their housebound evenings with humorous tall tales as he whittled an amusing collection of wooden ornaments. Enchanted with his stories and manual dexterity, Lisa hung on his every word and demonstration of wood-carving skill.

As Holly gazed at the proximity of their bright and dark heads from her place at the sewing machine, where she was hemming a set of napkins for Emma, she had to admit they'd grown thick as thieves. *He's the dad she's so sorely missed and needed,* she acknowledged. *I just hope that, when he decides to disappear again, it won't be too hard on her. She's already had to grieve the loss of one father.*

Compounded of longing and unrequited glances, her own relationship with Jake remained in a holding pattern. Though the estrangement caused by his unexplained absence had eased a bit, nothing of substance had been resolved between them. *If he doesn't tell me where he went and with whom, I'll always wonder,* Holly thought. *I'll never be able to place my trust in him.*

Even if they could get past the questions raised by his disappearance, she could think of other barriers to a serious relationship with Jake. First and foremost was her belief that principle couldn't be tailored to suit one's whims and desires. You either believed in something or you didn't. That being the case, she couldn't make unmarried love with him, whether or not Lisa was likely to be scandalized.

Try though she would to fathom them, Jake's feelings remained a mystery to her. He seemed to be biding his time, waiting patiently for her to forgive his absence, change her mind about him. She had the odd but persistent feeling he was leaving something unsaid. *I wish he'd spit it out, what-*

ever it is, even if it confirms my worst fears about him, she thought one chilly evening as their eyes met over the large white pine they'd cut down and dragged into the house to serve as their Christmas tree.

Polite, even friendly, but impassable as a wall without a door, the emotional standoff between them persisted through a tree-decorating session in which the three of them wrestled the majestic pine into its stand and hung its aromatic branches with strings of popcorn and cranberries, Jake's carved whimsies and Holly's fanciful if somewhat more traditional collection of ornaments.

Acquiring a life of its own, their arm's-length posture survived mornings of bitter cold as they hauled fodder to the stock, cocoonlike evenings of hot chocolate and Christmas carols on the radio.

Then, on a Saturday morning two weeks before Christmas, a fierce winter storm began to move across northern New Mexico and southern Colorado. Out until 4:00 p.m. distributing emergency feed to the cattle, many of which had huddled in a small box canyon for protection from the wind, Holly and Jake returned to the barn to discover that, though the other horses were fine, Lisa's beloved filly, Comet, wasn't herself. Usually bright and inquisitive, her eyes were dull and apathetic looking. She suffered from a runny nose. The food they'd placed in her trough that morning hadn't been touched.

His dark brows drawing together, Jake stroked the filly's nose and patted her neck. Her hide seemed uncommonly warm to the touch. "I think she's coming down with something," he speculated. "Maybe we ought to take her temperature."

By now, Holly was frowning, too. Ducking into the unoccupied stall she'd converted to a tack-and-supply room, she got out an equine thermometer and a jar of petroleum jelly. "Steady her, will you?" she asked, approaching Comet's hindquarters.

The thermometer measured Comet's temperature at 102.5 degrees. Normal range for a horse was between 99 and 101 degrees. She definitely had a fever.

"Put some rubbing alcohol and water in a bucket—fifty-fifty—and give her a rubdown, will you?" Holly requested. "I'm going into the house to call the vet."

As she trudged toward her front door through blowing snow, Holly saw to her relief that a four-wheel-drive vehicle had left rapidly blurring tire tracks in the driveway. Lars had managed to bring Lisa home from her Friday-night sleepover with Jane. She wouldn't be marooned at the Tørnquists' if the storm turned out to be as bad as weather forecasters were predicting.

Accustomed to spending every spare moment on Christmas crafts as the holiday approached, Lisa had flopped listlessly on the sofa. A new book by one of her favorite authors lay by her side, unopened. The hooded parka and mittens she'd worn to school the day before had been unceremoniously dumped in a nearby chair.

About to lecture her about the need to put her things away, Holly thought better of it. Instinct told her something wasn't right. "Hi, pumpkin...did you have a good time?" she asked instead, dropping a kiss on the girl's forehead.

Lisa shrugged. "Uh-huh," she said, sounding less than enthusiastic. "We made chocolate-chip cookies with Christmas sparkles."

And ate a few too many, Holly surmised, in addition to giggling and telling secrets half the night. "That sounds like fun," she said. "Sure you're feeling all right?"

"I'm okay."

Heading for the phone, Holly dialed the vet's number. To her chagrin, she got his message machine. "Ted, this is Holly Yarborough," she said after the beep. "It's roughly 4:30 p.m. Comet's running a fever. I know the weather's bad and you're probably busy, but could you possibly stop by on your way home? Or call? I'll be waiting to hear from you."

Lisa was at her elbow as she put down the receiver. "What's wrong with Comet?" she said urgently.

Holly placed a reassuring arm about the girl's shoulders. A strong believer in leveling with children when they asked for information, she conveyed the filly's temperature to her stepdaughter. "That's not terribly high," she explained. "But it isn't normal, either. I've got Jake sponging her down with cool water and alcohol."

Lisa's forehead was puckered with worry. "Can't we give her some of the antibiotics Dr. Ted gave you to put in the refrigerator?"

"Not without talking to him first."

"What if we can't reach him?"

"Then we'll decide."

The girl's eyes flashed with something of their customary purpose. "I want to help take care of her," she said, tugging on her boots.

Pocketing the portable phone, Holly accompanied Lisa back to the barn, where Jake was continuing to sponge the filly. After the relative heat of the house, the barn felt icy cold. While Lisa fussed over her beloved pet, stroking her neck and whispering in her ear, Holly swept an area free of straw and plugged in a space heater. With adequate precautions and someone around to keep an eye on it, sparks shouldn't be a problem, she thought.

Some twenty minutes later, the portable phone in her pocket shrilled. It was the vet, Dr. Ted Stephenson. "I got your message," he said in a harried voice. "Sorry, but it looks like I'm not going to make it over to your place this evening. I'm at the Masters ranch, near Antelope Crossing, about to conduct an emergency operation on Archie Masters's prize bull. The roads at this end of the county are close to impassable. What seems to be the trouble?"

Without wasting words, Holly described the filly's condition. "Sounds like equine flu," Ted Stephenson said. "I doubt if it's serious. Do you still have the penicillin I gave you? What about the tetracycline capsules?"

"Yes to both."

"Go ahead and give her fifteen cc's of the former. One of the capsules, too. It'll give her a boost."

Struggling back to the house through ever-deeper drifts and a steadily falling curtain of white, Holly removed a two-hundred-and-fifty milliliter bottle of penicillin from her refrigerator. The disposable syringes and tetracycline capsules Ted Stephenson had given her were on the top shelf of her spice and condiment cupboard. Pausing to take a jar of peanut butter from one of the other shelves, she filled a syringe with penicillin and returned the bottle to the refrigerator. A moment later, with her head bowed in the wind, she returned to Comet's stall.

Lisa winced slightly as Holly injected the penicillin directly into Comet's neck muscle. "Doesn't that hurt?" she asked.

Jake ruffled her hair. "No more than a pinch," he soothed.

His steadiness and affectionate way of dealing with Lisa will be sorely missed when he moves on to greener pastures, Holly thought. And that's not all. A hole will be torn in my heart big enough to accommodate a Mack truck.

Pushing down her personal feelings, she fished the tetracycline tablet from her pocket and removed the peanut butter jar's twist-off cap. "Here, Lisa . . . you can feed her the capsule," she said, intent on giving her stepdaughter something positive to do. "Just roll it into a nice, thick gob of peanut butter and offer it to her the way you would a carrot or piece of apple."

Accustomed to receiving treats from Lisa's hands, the filly took the tetracycline and peanut butter despite her lack of appetite. "Good job," Jake praised the girl. "When you become a vet someday, we won't have to call Dr. Stephenson. We'll have our own Dr. Yarborough right here on the premises."

The remark, which alluded to Lisa's dream of studying veterinary medicine, gave Holly fresh food for thought as Jake went back to sponging the filly's coat. Was it possible he planned to be around when Lisa was grown? Don't kid yourself, the skeptic in her scoffed. He was just trying to make her feel better.

Around 7:30 p.m., Holly took Comet's temperature again. It had dropped six-tenths of a degree. Though it was too soon to say so with any certainty, she appeared to be on the mend. Meanwhile, Lisa was drooping.

"Sure you're okay, baby doll?" Holly asked, smoothing the girl's unruly hair. "It's getting late. Do you want something to eat?"

Encouraged though she clearly was by the filly's progress, Lisa shook her head. "I'm not very hungry," she confessed. "I have a stomachache."

A worried glance passed between Jake and Holly. "Let me feel your head," Holly instructed.

Lightly pressed to Lisa's forehead, Holly's sensitive inner wrist confirmed her fears. Her stepdaughter had a fever. If she wasn't mistaken, it was in excess of one hundred degrees.

"Not you, too!" she said in alarm, zipping Lisa's parka up to her chin and tightening its drawstring hood about her face. "We've got to get you into bed at once. And call the doctor."

Outside the storm had gotten worse. Howling out of the north, the wind had buried the lane that connected the house with the county highway beneath an arctic terrain of snowdrifts. When they peered outside, they could barely make out any identifying landmarks.

Jake unplugged the heater. "I'll carry her," he volunteered, wrapping Lisa in a saddle blanket and scooping her up. "Grab hold of my jacket, Holly. I don't want us to get separated."

When she'd gone to fetch the antibiotics for Comet, Holly had left the kitchen lights on. Though their yellow glow wavered from moment to moment, occasionally disappearing altogether for a few seconds, it served as a beacon through the blinding curtain of snowflakes. In places, the drifts were up to their knees, making progress difficult. Clutching Lisa to his chest and sheltering her face from the wind, Jake slogged forward. Holly was right behind him, holding tight to his parka hem.

No previous sense of gratitude could compare with the one she felt when they reached her front porch. Wresting the door open against a particularly powerful gust, she stood back for Jake and Lisa to pass. The girl was whimpering as, like some kind of snow-encrusted guardian angel, he carried her to her room.

"Is it your stomach, sweetheart?" Holly asked, close behind him as he lowered her gently onto her bed.

Lisa nodded.

"Where does it hurt?"

Grimacing, the girl indicated her right side. Thoughts of appendicitis flickered through Holly's head. She dismissed them as borrowing trouble. Lisa's ailment was probably flu. It was making the rounds at her school.

"I'll undress her," she said to Jake, throwing off her jacket and unzipping Lisa's. "Get me some aspirin and a glass of water from the bathroom, will you? We're also going to need a bowl of ice water and a washcloth."

Tears of self-pity slipped down Lisa's cheeks as she swallowed the aspirin and Holly dressed her in a flannel nightgown. With several pillows plumped beneath her head and the covers pulled up to her chin, she didn't protest when Holly wrung the washcloth out in the ice water and bathed her forehead. "That feels good, Mommy," she whispered.

To Holly, Lisa's use of the familial term indicated just how sick she was. "That's good, pumpkin," she answered. "We'll have that nasty fever down in a little while. Take over for me, will you, Jake? I need to get in touch with the doctor."

She wasn't really surprised—just dismayed—when she discovered the phone was dead. Hopefully the company linemen would have it operating in the morning. In the meantime, they were on their own. Returning to Lisa's bedside, she signaled Jake without words that her effort had been unsuccessful.

Several nervous hours ensued, as Holly sponged her stepdaughter's overheated skin and Jake battled his way back and forth to the barn to check on the filly's progress. By 10:30 p.m., Comet was almost back to normal. In contrast, Lisa was verging on delirium. The right side of her stomach was swollen and rigid, arguing for Holly's discarded diagnosis.

"We have to do something, Jake," she said desperately, sharing her fears as she joined him for a moment out of Lisa's earshot. "But what? We can't call the doctor. And the roads are drifting over. Weather Service bulletins on the radio are urging people to stay indoors. If we try to drive her to the hospital in Larisson, we'll end up in a ditch . . . freeze to death beside the road someplace."

They could pack her in snow and hope her swollen appendix would shrink a little, Jake supposed. It was a radical solution, and maybe it wouldn't be needed. Holly's mention of the radio broadcast had jogged something in Jake's memory. "Wasn't that a shortwave set I saw in the attic when I brought down the storm windows?" he asked.

Holly wanted to kick herself. "Of *course!*" she acknowledged. "How could I have forgotten it? Clint bought it for exactly this sort of emergency. Unfortunately, I don't know how to operate it."

Jake did. Having learned to use a similar piece of equipment in Vietnam, he managed to reach a friendly ham operator who patched them through to the local emergency room. From what they told him about Lisa's condition, a doctor there agreed. Lisa probably had appendicitis.

"Our emergency chopper is out on another case. I'll dispatch it to you as soon as possible," he said. "Meanwhile, keep up what you're doing. You have good instincts."

With Jake's help and constant sponging, Holly was able to get Lisa's fever to recede somewhat. But she was still very hot. Abruptly, a message crackled on the shortwave set. "Be ready to evacuate your daughter in fifteen minutes."

Zipping Lisa's parka over her nightgown, they wrapped her in a blanket. As the rescue team's arrival time approached, Jake carried her to the door while Holly put on her own coat and mittens. Dear God . . . let my little girl be okay, Holly prayed as they waited for the rescue team. And thank you for Jake. Without him, we might not have made it.

Holly, her stepdaughter and the dark-haired ranch hand she loved fused in a three-way hug as the chopper came roaring out of the blizzard to land near their doorstep. Seconds later, the pilot and a medic were jumping out with a stretcher. "We won't need this," the latter said, handing the blanket they'd wrapped around Lisa back to Jake as he and his partner strapped the girl in place. "We have plenty of our own."

"Mommy?" Lisa asked, wide-eyed. "You're coming with me, aren't you? Please say yes...."

"Of course I am," Holly answered, daring the rescue team to contradict her.

The pilot glanced in her direction. "You're Mrs. Yarborough, the mother, right?" he said distractedly. "You can ride along." He nodded at Jake. "Sorry, we don't have room for him."

So quickly that it made her head spin, Holly was strapped into the emergency craft beside Lisa. She grasped the girl's hand and held it tightly, willing her appendix not to burst. Coming to life and whirling ever faster in the maelstrom of white, the helicopter's overhead blades began to emit their characteristic *chop-chop*. The engine noise was deafening as they lifted off the ground, rising straight up, like an elevator.

On the ground below, Lisa's blanket covering his head and shoulders to protect him from the driving snow, Jake was waving at them. "Don't worry," he shouted. "Lisa's going to be okay. I'll join you in town as soon as the roads are passable."

Wind snatched the words from his mouth. With all the din and the rapidly expanding distance, Holly guessed, she couldn't have caught them, anyway. Yet in her heart, she sensed their drift. Without him, this evening could have been far worse than it was, she thought again, leaning over to kiss Lisa's forehead.

* * *

Rushed to the surgical suite at Larisson Hospital for an emergency appendectomy, Lisa was transferred following her operation to a postanesthesia room. She was still groggy when Holly was allowed briefly to visit her. But her eyes were open.

"I'm going to be okay... aren't I, Mommy?" the girl asked.

This time it was Holly who had tears in her eyes. She didn't let them spill. "Absolutely good as new, pumpkin," she promised.

"You're going to stay right here?"

"The nurses can't watch over you properly if I'm in the way. If you need me, I'll be right down the hall, in the family waiting area."

Crashing on the Leatherette couch in the impersonally furnished lounge, Holly sorely missed Jake's presence. Now that Lisa was going to be all right, she'd given herself permission to shake a little. She wanted to rest her head on his shoulder—draw comfort from his strong, enveloping presence.

After checking on Lisa a second time, Holly returned to the waiting room couch. This time, she fell into an exhausted sleep. She didn't stir when a passing orderly returned and threw a spare blanket over her.

When she opened her eyes around 6:00 a.m., the snow seemed to have stopped. To her astonishment, Jake was there, a stubble of shadow beard darkening his chin, slouched in one of the armchairs with his back to the window. He was still wearing his outdoor parka, though he'd unzipped it. His long legs in their faded jeans were stretched out before him.

"So you're awake," he observed, getting to his feet.

Stiff from the cramped space where she'd been sleeping, Holly struggled to a sitting position. Though she was overjoyed to see him, her first thought was for her stepdaughter.

"Lisa?" she asked, rising also.

Jake gave her a tired smile. "Awake. And feeling much better. She's been assigned to a regular patient room. You can visit her if you want."

Relief coursed through Holly in a flood. "Thank God!" she exclaimed.

Courtesy of insights gained during the harrowing night they'd shared, the rift between them seemed the height of foolishness. Without compromising her responsibility to Lisa, she decided, she could lean on him for as long as he chose to stay around. She loved him, after all. If she didn't, she'd be sorry later. Propelled by instinct, she sought the sanctuary of his embrace, threading her arms around him beneath his worn, down-filled jacket. With a feeling of coming home, she blended into his body warmth.

Jake was totally undone. "Ah, Holly..." he whispered. "You can't possibly know how much I've longed to hold you this way."

Seconds later, their lips were meeting hungrily, greedily, easing their mutual deprivation. How had they managed to stay apart so long, when they needed each other so much?

When Holly learned the truth about his reasons for showing up on her doorstep and asking her for a job, Jake knew she'd be furious with him. He might find himself out in the cold again. Yet his defenses were down, his sense of practicality at a low ebb, thanks to the long, difficult night they'd just endured. He could think only of his need for her.

"Marry me," he begged, speaking words he'd never spoken to anyone. "Holly, darling...I love you so much."

Chapter Seven

He was her hired hand. And the man she loved. She knew everything about him. And nothing. Reason suggested she'd be crazy to marry him—a man with no money of his own and seemingly no ambition except, possibly, to gain a stake in the ranch Clint had put in her name with the express purpose that, someday, she'd bequeath it to Lisa.

The thought wasn't worthy of him and, instinctively, Holly knew it. Yet she had to protect her stepdaughter's interests. In addition, she still didn't know where Jake had gone when he'd been absent from Honeycomb those two weeks. *Had* there been another woman in his life during the time she'd known him? Did he have an ex-wife and children someplace?

She couldn't bring herself to ask. Stalling, she took refuge in a question. "Are you...serious about this?" she asked.

It was Jake's moment of truth. Though he'd never entertained the idea before, marriage with Holly was something he'd come to want with all his heart. With the thought, the burden of his deception grew heavier. If he told Holly who he really was and what he was doing in her life, she'd refuse to marry him. She'd almost certainly kick him off her property. Yet she deserved to know the truth.

As tired as he was, and more bereft of his acute facility for predicting what others would do than at any time he could remember, he managed to convince himself that, once they were engaged—no, wed and happy together—her spasm of anger on learning the truth would quickly play itself out.

We're perfect for each other, he thought. Not to have a life together would be criminal. I want to make her heart sing again, as she has mine.

"I've never been more serious about anything in my life, darlin'," he said, his untold secret a lump in his throat as he traced the shape of her mouth with one gentle fingertip.

Aching at the tempered sweetness of the gesture and bursting with love at his declaration, Holly had sufficient unanswered questions to be scared to death. Putting them on hold, she withdrew a little. "Mind if we talk about this a little later?" she asked. "Right now, I want to check on Lisa."

Eager as he was for an answer, Jake wasn't offended. "Okay by me," he said. "Mind if I tag along?"

Holly slipped her hands into his larger ones. "Of course not," she answered. "After last night, Lisa and I owe you a great deal. I know how much you care about us."

The girl's surgeon had just finished examining her when they entered her room. "Ah, Mrs. Yarborough," he said. "I'm glad you're here. This young lady of yours is doing just fine. If there aren't any complications, she'll be free to go home day after tomorrow." He paused, glancing at Jake. "I take it you're *Mr.* Yarborough," he said.

Lisa giggled at the misnomer, though it caused her to clutch her side. For her part, Holly was blushing. She was grateful for Jake's nonchalance as he shrugged off the question. In her opinion, most men wouldn't have.

"I'm Jake McKenzie," he told the surgeon in a friendly tone, declining to explain his relationship to them.

As expected, Lisa got a little teary when it was time for them to go. Still, raised on a ranch, she knew from experience that they had to return home and check on the animals.

"You'll call and let me know how Comet's doing, won't you, Mommy?" she asked.

Holly bent to give the girl a hug. "Of course I will," she promised. "By now, she's probably yearning for some of the carrots and apples you always give her. Since you can't take care of that today, Jake and I will do it for you."

Though Jake's proposal and Holly's delay in giving him an answer were on both their minds as they got into his truck and started for home, neither of them brought up the subject. He'd decided to give her as much time as she needed, now that he'd spoken his piece. And, sensing that, she'd decided to take it. As a result, their scraps of conversation were confined to the storm and the massive pileup of snow on both sides of the highway.

Their route took them past the Tørnquist ranch, where sixty-five-year-old Lars was attempting to plow his driveway. As a by-product of the effort to make way for traffic, the county snowplow had thrown up an eight-foot-high barrier of white at his gate. He was obviously having a difficult time removing it.

Meanwhile, Jake's truck had Holly's snow blade attached to the front. He'd had to borrow it in order to make it out of her driveway once the highways were clear.

"Mind if I stop and help?" he asked. "I can run you up to the house for coffee with Emma while you wait."

It was the sort of neighborly thing folks did for one another in the valley, and sweet of Jake to offer. Holly had worried a bit about Lars overdoing it of late. Besides, she was only too glad of the chance to talk with Emma, who was a kind of surrogate mother to her.

"That's a great idea," she said.

Clearly guessing Jake's purpose when he dropped Holly off at her door and, making a U-turn, returned to the spot where Lars was working, Emma threw open her front door before Holly had a chance to knock.

"How nice of Jake to stop and help," she said, welcoming Holly into her house. "Snow removal is such hard work and Lars isn't getting any younger. Come...let's talk in the kitchen. I've got the coffee on."

They settled at Emma's maple dinette, which fitted cozily into the embrace of a large bay window. As promised, the coffee was steaming hot as Holly's neighbor poured it into blue willow china cups. So were the double-blueberry muffins that had just emerged from the oven.

As they sipped Emma's steaming brew, Jane wandered in from the family room. "Where's Lisa?" she asked. "Why didn't you bring her, Mrs. Yarborough?"

The question prompted a complete rendition of the previous night's events, ending with Holly and Jake's visit to Lisa's hospital room a short time earlier. Holly left out just one newsworthy detail—Jake's marriage proposal.

In response, Emma was shaking her head. Jane was wide-eyed to learn about her best friend's illness. "How awful that must have been for Lisa!" the girl exclaimed when Holly fell silent. "Would it be all right if I called her, Gram? I could ask the nurse to give her a message if she's sleeping or something."

"The phones are working again?" Holly interjected.

Emma nodded. "They came back on around 8:00 a.m. Okay with you if Jane phones the hospital?"

Holly gave her permission. A minute or so later, the distant murmur of Jane's voice reached them as she spoke into the telephone receiver in her bedroom down the hall. Apparently, Lisa was awake and able to take calls, because Jane settled in for a lengthy chat.

"So," Emma remarked, turning her attention back to Holly, "you had quite an adventure during the storm. After hearing about what happened, I'm going to insist we get a shortwave radio."

Holly nodded her approval. "I think that would be a good idea." She paused. "Emma...I was, umm, wondering about something."

Her curiosity clearly aroused, the older woman regarded Holly expectantly.

On the verge of asking for Emma's opinion of Jake, Holly took a different tack. "What did the girls eat Friday night? Lisa said she and Jane made chocolate-chip cookies. How many did they eat?"

Emma rolled her eyes. "Quite a few more than I would have allowed them to, had I known about it. Once the cookies were out of the oven, I went to bed. Lars was up, doing book work, but he didn't pay much attention to them. Neither of us had a clue until Saturday morning, when I saw how few cookies were left." She smiled. "Kids Jane's age can be quite a handful for grandparents!"

"Do you think their gorging could have caused Lisa's appendicitis?"

Emma shrugged. "I doubt it, though I suppose an overload of sweets could have made it worse." Hesitating, she regarded Holly silently for a moment. "Why do I have the feeling you want to tell me something important?" she asked.

Feeling as if her friend and neighbor was adept at reading her mind, Holly decided to level with her. "Jake has asked me to marry him," she said, keeping her voice down so Jane wouldn't overhear.

Emma's round, weather-beaten face creased in a smile. "How wonderful! I'm so happy for you," she said, reaching across the table to squeeze Holly's hand. "Naturally, I can't help wishing it could have been Nels. But I never really expected that. It's easy to see you and Jake love each other."

Had they been that obvious? Holly blushed. "I haven't given him an answer yet," she admitted. "I have some doubts. To begin with, I know next to nothing about his past. Frankly, it worries me that someone as smart and capable as he seems to be has contented himself with the life of a wandering ranch hand. If ranching is what he loves, why hasn't he found a way to buy a place of his own? Doesn't he have any ambition? I hate myself for thinking such thoughts. But it *has* occurred to me that he might see me and Lisa as a means to advance himself."

The worst was out and Emma didn't seem shocked. Instead, she appeared thoughtful. "You know him better than I do, dear," she said at last, throwing the question back into Holly's lap. "But it seems to me that a man's behavior is the best road map of what's in his heart. Jake's been good...*to* you and *for* you. He clearly dotes on Lisa. And he seems like a solid person. Anyone can have reversals in their life, and maybe he did. If you have questions, why don't you put them to him?"

Holly was afraid that if she aired her reservations to Jake, it would be all over with them. Despite the paucity of his assets, she suspected, he was a proud man. Wounded over her failure to trust him, he might walk out of her life for good. And that would kill her. She didn't know what to do.

A short time later, Jake and Lars came in to stoke up on coffee. The four of them talked awhile—mostly about the storm, the possibility that they might need to airlift feed if additional snow fell before a thaw and the need for the Tørnquists to get a shortwave radio. Though Emma's eyes held a new benevolence as she gazed at Holly and her dark-haired cowboy, she didn't betray by word or deed that she knew about Jake's proposal.

At last, Jake got to his feet. "We'd better go home... check on the animals and have breakfast," he suggested.

Holly quickly agreed.

The phone was ringing as they stomped the snow off their boots on her front porch and entered the house. Plaintive as a calf that had been separated from its mother, Lisa's voice came over the line when Holly picked it up.

"Mommy?" her stepdaughter said. "You sound so far away. I'm feeling awfully lonesome. And it doesn't hurt anywhere... at least, not much. Do you think I could come home early?"

"I'm not sure, baby doll," Holly replied. "We don't want to do anything that would impede your recovery. I suppose I could phone your doctor this afternoon and explore the idea."

"*Would* you?" The girl's words positively jumped with enthusiasm. "It's so boring up here! And the food isn't very good. How is Comet doing?"

Forced to report Jake had been helping Lars plow his driveway and they hadn't been out to the barn yet, Holly signaled him it was likely to be a lengthy mother-daughter conversation.

She hadn't given him the semblance of an answer yet. But Jake was hopeful. Giving her an indulgent grin, he volunteered to see to the animals by himself.

Some twenty minutes later, after promising Lisa for the second time that she'd call the surgeon's office, Holly managed to end the call. She and Jake desperately needed something to eat. With the exception of several blueberry muffins at Emma's, neither of them had eaten since Saturday noon, when they'd taken a break from distributing feed to wolf down some hot coffee and a couple of ham sandwiches.

Taking a quick shower and putting on fresh jeans and a clean sweater, she returned to the kitchen, where she whipped up an omelet and the chicken-fried steak she'd planned to serve the night before. As she dished them up on a pair of heated plates and placed them on a serving tray covered with a blue-and-white striped dish towel, she paused to reflect that things had changed dramatically between her and Jake. Like it or not, his proposal and confession of love for her had caused her to lower her guard.

The way he'd helped and protected them the night before also had a lot to do with it. Love is more action than declaration, she thought. That being the case, what can I do for him?

The answer came from the deepest, most instinctive part of herself. *You could learn to trust him.*

Tugging on her boots and zipping up her parka, she carried the meal she'd repaired out to the barn. "Breakfast...with a little of last night's unmade supper thrown in," she announced with a smile that didn't quite hide the excitement and uncertainty she felt.

Jake emerged from Comet's stall. His beard-roughened face in shadow, he looked dead serious. For most of the night after she and Lisa had left in the chopper, and again during their drive back to Honeycomb that morning, he'd agonized over the secret he hadn't shared with her.

Characteristically, he was determined to get what he wanted, come hell or high water—a home with her and her little girl. Gently taking the tray from her hands, he set it aside on a bale of hay and took Holly in his arms.

"Say you'll marry me," he demanded, crushing her to him in a fierce embrace. "Life without you wouldn't be worth a damn now that I know what we could have together."

Briefly his words stirred her fears that he might be trying to take advantage of them even as they deeply warmed her heart. Which way of looking at things would win out? For Holly's inner woman, there wasn't any contest.

"Though I wasn't willing to admit it earlier, I love you, too," she confided. "If you're serious about making a life with us, I'd be proud and happy to marry you."

To her, he was just a down-at-the-heels cowboy. Unlike most of the women he'd previously known, she'd acknowledged her love for him without knowing anything about his Juris Doctorate or considering his tax bracket. Meanwhile, with her valiant heart and high standards, her sweet, giving nature, she was the biggest prize a man could want.

Ecstatic, humbled, he pushed down the guilt he felt over deceiving her about his connections to Dutch and crushed her mouth with his. Beneath her jacket and the sweater she'd pulled on without bothering to fasten on a bra, his big, callused hands were caressing and claiming her. Erect and ready to prove his love, his manhood was pressing against her lower stomach.

Holly's response was like an avalanche. From deep within, a tide of longing welled up, crying out to be satisfied. What does it matter if we're not married yet? she rationalized. We soon *will* be. I don't want to wait to welcome him inside me, become his lover in every sense.

This time, it was Jake who tugged them back from the brink. She was ready to give him everything. And he couldn't let her do it.

"What's wrong?" she asked, the dark velvet of her pupils swallowing up the gray of her irises.

The answer to her question was there in his face. "Nothing, my dearest darlin'," he whispered, encircling her tightly as he kissed the tip of her nose. "I just think we ought to defer making love out of respect for your feelings. Of course, that means you'll have to marry me pretty damn quick."

It was what she wanted, too. "What would you say to Christmas Eve?" she suggested, feeling incredibly sheltered and cherished as she smiled up at him. "That's less than two weeks from today."

"I can't think of anything I'd rather do than marry you at Christmas," Jake said.

More kisses followed, hot but careful not to nudge past the boundaries they'd set. At last, stomach hunger got the better of them. Laughing together over their tendency to forget practical matters when they were in each other's arms, they carried the breakfast tray back into the house. Thanks to their neglect, the omelet was a congealed mess. However, the steak was salvageable. Reheated, sliced thin and doused with barbecue sauce from the refrigerator, it made excellent sandwiches.

When she phoned Lisa's surgeon that afternoon, Holly learned that he'd stopped by to see the girl again. "She's mending nicely," he related. "But then children usually bounce back from these things. Of course, you know she's angling to come home early. This afternoon's still out of the question, but tomorrow's a possibility, provided you have the time and inclination to wait on her hand and foot for a couple of days."

With Jake available to tend the stock, Holly felt free to accept. She phoned Lisa with the news, apprising Jake of her decision at the dinner table. "Naturally, that means less privacy for us," she admitted. "But with Lisa so lonesome and feeling better..."

Savoring a mouthful of Holly's spicy Taos chili, Jake patted her hand. "You did the right thing," he said, the laugh lines deepening beside his mouth. "The way you light my fire, we *need* a chaperon."

Though Jake managed to keep his promise to himself, they did several things that evening they wouldn't have dreamed of doing if Lisa were around. Adding several logs to the fire and dialing a mellow "oldies" station on the radio, he settled on the couch with Holly in the curve of his shoulder. As they kissed, talked and kissed some more, they planned to hold their wedding at home and discussed whom to invite. Since her closest family members were second cousins she hadn't seen since the third grade, Holly's contingent would consist of neighbors and friends. To her chagrin, Jake claimed he didn't have anyone in mind.

"Like you, I don't have any close family," he explained. "And few true friends, if you want the truth. None of them live around here. I'll be happy if it's just us, Lisa, the Tørnquists, and anyone else you want to invite."

It would have to do. Willing to take him without some of the blanks filled in, Holly worked up her courage to ask what she considered to be two essential questions. Had Jake been married before? Ever fathered a child? Or children?

His answer was no to both questions. "Though I never found anyone I wanted to marry until I met you, I always thought I'd like being a husband and father someday,'' he said, lifting Holly's left hand and lightly pressing it to his lips. ''Being around you and Lisa has only confirmed that feeling a hundredfold. Though we'll be a family cobbled together by happenstance, with a child who isn't related by blood to either of us, I can't imagine being part of one that would be more satisfying to my soul. I'll be honored to be Lisa's father by marriage—and your husband in every sense.''

In honor of Holly's principles, she and Jake didn't make love that night. Yet they agreed it would have been asking too much of them not to sleep together. Outside, the temperature had dropped into the single digits and, with Holly still saving on heating costs, the room was positively polar. Yet they didn't suffer from any lack of warmth. Deep in each other's arms beneath Holly's down coverlet and several layers of woolen blankets, they luxuriated in each other's body heat as they kissed, touched and fantasized about what the future might hold.

With her most pressing questions about Jake's past laid to rest and no idea of the secret he was keeping from her, Holly's imagined scenarios were all of blue skies, sunlight and summer weather, horseback riding in the mountains with the man and girl she loved. As they had on a fall day in the not-so-distant past, they'd picnic within view of snow-covered peaks, run laughing through a meadow full of wildflowers.

Afterward, they'd come home, eat, listen to music on the radio as she sewed, Jake whittled and Lisa read or worked on one of her craft projects. Lovers at last, she and Jake would sleep together. Though her fantasy was a simple one—not what most people would consider glamorous or exotic, she suspected—it sounded like heaven on earth to her.

Happier than he'd ever dreamed possible, Jake couldn't stop thinking in a more somber vein. What would Holly do when he finally was forced to tell her the truth about himself? Would she ever forgive him for his deception? She has a right to know what she's getting into, and with whom, his conscience argued. If you don't tell her *now*, her trust in you is sadly misplaced.

Aching to reveal the truth and, in the best of all possible outcomes, receive her forgiveness, he couldn't bring himself to take the risk. Though he upbraided himself for his lack of courage, he decided to wait until after they were married before broaching the subject. Once we've spoken our vows, it'll be harder for her to kick me out, he reasoned. Yet he knew that the longer he waited, the greater his offense would be, the heavier his burden.

He was also thinking about Lisa and the need to make her feel safe and loved in their new arrangement. As he and Holly dressed for the trip into Larisson to pick her up the following morning, he advanced the somewhat courtly notion of asking the girl's permission to marry her.

"You mean . . . propose 'daughtership' to her?" Holly asked, a dimple flashing beside her mouth.

Jake grinned, too. His blue eyes betrayed only a minimal worry that he might be rejected. "In a sense, the three of us will be marrying one another," he explained. "I want Lisa to be as enthusiastic as we are about our new life together."

Holly's redheaded stepdaughter was dangling her legs over the edge of her hospital bed, fiddling with some paper dolls one of the nurses had given her, when they arrived. "You're here!" she exclaimed in delight, jumping to her feet and giving Holly a hug. "Did you remember to bring my clothes?"

"Here they are," Holly answered, handing Lisa the duffel bag she used for her overnights with Jane. "By the way...as soon as you're dressed, Jake would like to talk to you about something."

About to dash into the small adjacent bathroom so she could change into her jeans, sweater and parka as fast as possible, Lisa hesitated. She glanced from Jake to her stepmother. "What about?" she demanded, clearly sensing something important was at stake.

"The fact that I want to marry Holly." To Lisa's obvious astonishment, Jake went down before her on bended knee. "I won't do it without your approval, pumpkin," he said. "Could you handle having me as Holly's husband...and your new stepdad?"

Lisa gaped at him. "You already asked her, didn't you?" she speculated, recovering. "And she told you *yes.*"

Jake nodded. Beside him, Holly held her breath.

Again there was silence. "It wouldn't be like you were taking my real dad's place, would it?" Lisa asked slowly.

"No, it wouldn't," Jake agreed.

"But...you could have a spot of your own."

His heart turned over at the girl's wisdom. "It's what I want, sweetheart," he whispered. "More than anything."

Like the sun at its zenith, dispelling dark clouds, a smile lit her freckled countenance. "Then it's okay with me," she said shyly. "In fact, I think it's a cool idea."

Seconds later, the three of them were caught in a fierce embrace.

Chapter Eight

When they phoned Emma with the news, she responded with delight and an invitation. "Have the ceremony at our house," she suggested. "We have more space. A bigger Christmas tree, thanks to the height of our living room. And several dozen candles left over from our celebration of St. Lucia's Day. You'll be able to concentrate on getting married without the burden of entertaining. Afterward, Lisa can stay over with Jane, so you'll have a proper wedding night."

Though at first they protested that it would be too much work for her, ultimately Jake and Holly accepted. They had to agree that the huge stone fireplace in the Tørnquists' living room, which was always elaborately decorated at Christmastime, was the ideal backdrop for their exchange of vows.

Following the snowstorm that accompanied Lisa's airlift to the hospital, the weather turned sunny, dry and cold. Jake assumed a greater role in caring for the animals and performing maintenance tasks around the ranch while Holly concentrated on getting ready for the wedding and finishing up her Christmas presents. In her spare moments while Jake was out-of-doors, she was fashioning a bulky sweater for him from a deep blue yarn that matched his eyes.

By now, her long-legged cowboy had won her trust in addition to her affection. After two lonely years spent running the ranch without Clint's help and raising Lisa on her own, she'd found a man to love. And what a man he was—tall, sexy and remarkably nurturing. Each time they kissed, his mouth seared her very soul. Over and over, as she imagined them setting a seal on their love, the yarn would slacken in her fingers.

She had wedding preparations to complete, though Emma would be in charge of the hostessing. First and foremost, she needed a dress. What she *had,* as a typical hard-working rancher, was a closet full of jeans and sweaters, and not much money in her bank account. Still, she had an idea in mind that was both affordable and full of sentiment.

Near the end of Lisa's first week home, as the girl napped on the living room couch with the novel *Black Beauty* open beside her, Holly disappeared into her bedroom and lifted the lid of her grandmother's cedar chest. Yes... there they were, Grandma Peterson's wedding dress and veil, preserved in layers of tissue beneath a stack of hand-embroidered tablecloths. The former Mabel Tørgilson had wed Olaf Peterson in 1928, five years before giving birth to Holly's mother, and the white, ankle-length dress reflected it.

Made of clinging silk peau de soie over a matching slip in a whisper-weight version of the same fabric, it had long sleeves and a modest neckline decorated with seed pearls. The veil was attached to a head-hugging satin cap, also decorated with pearls and trimmed with hand-appliquéd swirls of silk soutache braid. She hadn't worn them when she and

Clint had pledged their troth before a justice of the peace, considering them too formal for that occasion, and she'd regretted it ever afterward.

Now she had another chance.

To be married in the flapper-era outfit would be to carry on a family tradition, as her mother had worn it, too. It would also save her money she could ill afford to spend. It can't be allowed to matter that Mom and Dad's marriage ended in divorce, she thought. Mine and Jake's won't, and that's what counts. Though the arbiters of such things might have considered her grandmother's gown hopelessly dated, Holly thought it exquisite. To her, the echoes it summoned of other times and places only added to its mystique.

When she modeled it before the pier glass in the living room, it fit as if it had been custom-made for her. Taking off the cap and veil, and unbraiding her hair so that its waist-length tresses descended in waves about her shoulders, she surveyed herself again. With her hair loose, the ensemble took on an almost medieval air. Humming a ballad the musicians had played as she and Jake had danced together at the Cunninghams' party, she regarded herself with pleasure. I'll wear my jeans to drive to the Tørnquists' so my bridal garments won't get wrinkled, she thought.

Jake wouldn't see her in the outfit until she put it on in one of her neighbors' guest bedrooms. But he heard about it from Lisa. Realizing it would mean a great deal to Holly if he dressed appropriately for the occasion as well, he made a quick trip into Pagosa Springs to buy a suit off the rack. Though he was tempted, he could hardly step forward to claim her hand in one of the custom-made suits that was currently languishing in his Durango closet. If Holly asked how he'd managed to afford the dark jacket and slacks he bought in a men's discount store, he decided, he'd simply tell her that he'd saved up his paychecks.

The problem of her wedding attire resolved, Holly turned her attention to Lisa's. It, too, proved to be a frugal, easy choice. The red velveteen dress she'd made the girl for the Cunninghams' party was perfect. Despite the clash of shades with Lisa's mass of carroty curls, the dress looked good on her. And she loved the color. I wonder who we can get to take some photographs, Holly mused, imagining the tableau they'd make. Maybe Tom Tibbets can do it. I've heard he's handy with a camera.

At last, it was Christmas Eve—the fourth shortest day of the year. From first light, the sky had been cloudy and gray. Now, as they made their final preparations, the sun was setting behind a bank of darkening clouds. A light veil of snow began to fall. Initially so fine that they were barely visible, the snowflakes grew huge and lacy, like children's paper-lace cutouts.

Plagued by a mild case of nerves, yet at bottom secure in the knowledge that her marriage to Jake was meant, Holly had packed her best underwear, nylons and pearl earrings in an alligator-embossed train case that had belonged to her as a girl. Her gown and veil were on padded hangers, carefully swathed in plastic dry-cleaner's bags.

She'd splurged on a pair of white satin, low-heeled slippers for herself and a gold locket for Lisa, who might feel left out if she didn't have something new, as well. I hope the spring calving is good so our finances won't be so tight, she thought as she smoothed her grandmother's wedding gown through its transparent covering. Lisa deserves a treat now and then. Maybe we'll do better with Jake to help out from now on instead of a series of uncaring drifters.

"Holly... hurry up! We're going to be late!"

An excited tug from Lisa's hand accompanied the urgent request. Unlike her stepmother, the girl had elected to wear her best for the brief journey, though she'd bowed to circumstances and tucked her black patent flats into her overnight bag. She was ready except for the act of putting on her coat—and fairly dancing with impatience.

Gathering up her things, Holly followed Lisa into the living room and promptly caught her breath. Instead of his usual jeans, sweater and flannel shirt, which were the extent of his wardrobe as far as she knew, Jake was wearing a dark suit, white shirt and tie. A pair of black tooled-leather cowboy boots she hadn't seen before peeked out from beneath his trouser legs. He'd tucked a sprig of her namesake botanical in his buttonhole.

Smiling at her astonishment, he gave her a little salute.

"Where...where did you get that outfit?" she stammered, too smitten with the way he looked to articulate what she felt.

Casting a twinkling, blue-eyed glance at Lisa, who'd clearly been in on the secret of his upgraded wardrobe, he kissed the tip of Holly's nose. "I saved my pay and went on a little shopping spree," he claimed.

"Well, you look wonderful."

The blue eyes got merrier. "Thank you very much."

By now, Lisa was bundled to face the elements. Zipping on their parkas and scooping up several gaily wrapped Christmas presents for Emma, Lars and Jane, Holly and Jake followed her out the door. The soles of their boots squeaked on the tightly packed snow as they hurried to Holly's truck, which Jake had dashed out earlier to leave warming in the driveway.

When we return home, we'll be married, Holly thought, overwhelmed by the powerful love and closeness contained in the cab of her modest pickup as they settled in for their brief journey. Though she couldn't prove it in any objective sense, she felt certain she was the luckiest woman in the world.

As always at Christmastime, her neighbors' ranch house was ablaze with St. Lucia candles, the warm glow of firelight and what seemed a hundred strings of Christmas bulbs. The bulbs were twined about an oversize, aromatic Christmas tree. Positioned beside the massive stone hearth that would serve as the backdrop for their wedding vows, it filled the air with its strong evergreen scent. Christmas carols were playing softly on the stereo.

They were a few minutes late. Holly barely had time to duck into one of the guest bedrooms to dress before the first guests arrived. As she shed her jeans, she silently thanked Emma for setting out every item she conceivably might want—lotion, tissue, a pincushion full of pins, even a pair of panty hose in her slender size in case she snagged the stockings she'd brought.

Taking off her sweater and putting on her nylons and lacy garter belt, Holly removed her wedding slip from its protective covering and shimmied it over her head. The dress came next, cool like its matching undergarment from the brisk December air.

For once, she'd decided, she'd wear makeup. Before putting on her veil, she sat on the padded bench at the dressing table to smooth on a light blusher and add a trace of mascara, a dab of lipstick. Next came her pearl earrings, which were shaped like tiny teardrops. Unfastening her braid, she brushed out the heavy blond length of her hair so that it fell liquid about her shoulders.

Last of all, she settled her cap and veil into place. As she did so, her eyes caught and held those of her alter ego in the mirror. Tonight, you and the handsome cowboy who appeared at your gate in October will be husband and wife, she acknowledged with a little shiver of happiness.

She could only imagine the ecstasy of making love to him. Her sexual encounters with Clint—the only ones she'd

known to date—had generated more relaxed togetherness
than heat. Happy enough, she'd never known soul-deep
contentment. From the kisses she and Jake had exchanged,
she knew her experience with him would fall into a completely different category.

By now, the chatter of guests in the Tørnquists' living
room had reached an expectant pitch. Tapping lightly on the
door, Lisa slipped into the room. Her mouth opening to
deliver some message or other, she stopped dead in her
tracks and stared. "You're so beautiful, Holly!" she said
after a moment.

Her heart overflowing with love for the world at large,
Holly held out her arms. For once the girl hesitated to come
into them. "I don't want to crush your dress," Lisa protested.

Holly shook her head. Though Lisa hadn't grown to the
maturity of birth beneath her heart, she considered the girl
to be her own in every other sense. Lisa and Jake would
form a similar bond, she hoped. "Don't you know I *want*
it to have that kind of crease, sweetheart?" she asked.

The hug they exchanged was heartfelt, an unspoken vow
that the charmed circle of Holly's love for her husband-to-
be would always include Lisa and bring them even closer
together. Emerging from it, the girl announced that the
Tørnquists' minister had arrived. "We're ready to start," she
said, sounding serious and extremely grown-up. "If you are,
too, I'll tell Mrs. Baake she can play the wedding march."

Imogen Baake, the minister's wife, had been enlisted to
play the Tørnquists' upright piano throughout the service.

Taking a deep breath, Holly didn't answer for a moment. It was her last chance to back out, if that was what she
wanted. I've only known Jake a couple of months, she
thought. And, though he's told me a few stories about his
boyhood and tour of duty in Vietnam, much of his history

is still unknown to me. Whenever I've tried to get him to fill in the blanks or discuss the string of jobs he's held, he's found a way to shrug off my questions. What am I doing, marrying him?

On the verge of a belated panic attack, she remembered Emma's words of wisdom. Hadn't her motherly neighbor opined that a man's actions were the best key to what was in his heart? And hadn't she agreed with that assessment?

From his first afternoon at Honeycomb, Jake had been decent, loving and protective of both of them. Without knowing every detail of his past, she could afford to trust him. "You can tell her I'm ready," she directed.

Jake was talking with Lars by the fireplace when someone switched off the stereo. Wide-eyed at the gravity of what they were about to do, Lisa slipped her hand into his. Emotions fierce and tremulous pierced him to the quick as Imogen Baake began to play the age-old processional.

Somewhere beyond the sudden quiet that swept the guests, a door opened. Holly appeared in the shadows of the bedroom hall. After a slight hesitation, she entered the living room. The buzz of admiring whispers that greeted her caused twin spots of color to bloom in her cheeks.

In her antique dress, with her unbraided hair cascading about her shoulders, she was so fresh, so radiant, that Jake's heart turned over in his chest. As he stepped forward to take her hand and lead her back to the fireplace, he could scarcely believe his luck. What had he done to deserve such happiness, the love and trust that were shining in her face?

God knew he loved her with all his heart, that he was ready a thousand times over to shed his bachelorhood like a worn-out coat. Yet by his failure to tell her the full truth about himself and the mission that had brought him to her door, he'd violated her trust. How did you let things get this far? he asked himself. But he knew the answer well enough.

If he'd told her everything, the love they shared would never have had a chance to blossom.

He'd just have to beg her forgiveness at the appropriate moment. Maybe I can make it up to her by forcing Dutch to see how good she is for Lisa, he kidded himself, his hand tightening about Holly's as they faced the minister. Maybe the family we're cementing today won't have to fall apart.

Holding out her hand to Lisa, Holly drew the girl against her side as Elton Baake began to read the wedding service. Though Jake's voice nearly broke with emotion when it was time for him to say his vows, hers floated clear and true into the pine-scented hush that filled the Tørnquists' living room. But it was Lisa's, "Yes!" when—per their instructions—Elton Baake asked if she took Jake and Holly to be her parents till death did them part that carried the day.

"Did I do something wrong, Mommy?" the girl whispered, embarrassed at the indulgent ripple of amusement her response had evoked.

Holly shook her head. "You were perfect, pumpkin."

Seconds later, the minister was asking Jake for the ring. Assuming Jake couldn't afford to purchase one, Holly hadn't brought up the subject. They'd said nothing about a ring to the minister. Now she gaped as her groom retrieved a worn gold band set with garnets from his pocket.

"With this ring, which was my mother's wedding band, I thee wed," he said with unabashed sentimentality, causing her eyes to mist.

There wasn't any way he could have sized the ring for her finger. Yet it fit as if it had been custom made for her. Jake, Jake, she thought, lifting her gaze to his. Can you ever forgive me for doubting you?

Goose bumps brushed Holly's skin as the minister pronounced them husband and wife. It was time for their nuptial embrace. How big, how solid, Jake is, she thought as she put her arms around him and offered up her mouth. A rock that will see me through any trouble. The beloved object of my desire.

Though it held just a hint of the passion she knew ran hot in him, Jake's swooping confiscation of her mouth was all-consuming. Its warmth flooded her soul, easing its places of greatest loneliness. *You are loved,* it seemed to promise. *Whatever lies ahead, we'll weather it.*

How long they stood there, communing in a way that blurred the physical and the spiritual, she couldn't have said afterward—just that time seemed to stand still and the room might as well have been empty of wedding guests.

Lisa's urgent poke in their ribs returned them to their senses. "You guys are embarrassing me," she whispered.

The most sacred moments of the ceremony having passed, the guests applauded when Jake widened his embrace to include the blushing ten-year-old. In response, they hugged some more, the three-way tie that united them in an almost tangible presence.

"Time for a toast," Lars proposed in his mostly Americanized Swedish accent and suddenly the ceremony was complete. Several of Holly's neighbors had offered to tend bar, and champagne corks quickly began popping. Without consulting them, it turned out, the Tørnquists had provided enough of the celebratory beverage for several rounds of good wishes. Even Lisa and Jane got tiny sips.

Our married life has begun, Holly thought wonderingly, her earlier tension evaporating into smiles and hugs as friends and neighbors surrounded them to pump Jake's hand and kiss her cheek. Behind them, Christmas lights sparkled on lavishly decorated boughs. Gradually the crescendo of talk and laughter intensified. As Emma and Lars invited everyone to partake of the caraway-and-onion meatballs in sour cream and other Scandinavian delicacies that waited on the buffet, Imogen Baake began to play traditional Christmas carols.

Singing and even a bit of dancing followed, along with the pleasurable opening of wedding gifts. However, the reception wasn't scheduled to run very late. The Tørnquists and their guests had last-minute preparations to make for their own family celebrations of Christmas. Besides, Holly and Jake were eager to start their honeymoon.

Her veil removed and carefully placed inside her train case along with her satin slippers, Holly pulled on her cowboy boots and zipped her parka over the top half of her wedding dress. In that outlandish getup, she hugged Emma and Lars good-night. "Thank you, *thank you both*... for everything!" she exclaimed, barely able to contain the enormous gratitude she felt. "What you did for us was so wonderful...."

"It was our pleasure, dear." Emma beamed. "It's good to see you so happy."

Lars nodded in agreement, his weather-beaten face creasing in a broad smile. "We benefited, too," he claimed. "We'll always own a little piece of your happiness."

The acceptance and friendship Holly's neighbors had accorded him—for the man he was, not the money and credentials that had seemed so important to everyone he'd met in his legal career—thoroughly touched Jake's heart. Together with Holly's and Lisa's affection, they'd brought him solidly to earth in a place he'd begun to call his own. If only he could keep them....

He'd move heaven and earth if that's what it took. His only fear was that, once he leveled with Holly about his relationship to Dutch, his boundless love for her might not be enough.

"Emma, Lars... I'll never be able to repay you for your kindness," he said soberly.

"Yes, you can." Lars gave his shoulder a squeeze. "You can take good care of this special lady."

With hugs and kisses for Lisa and anyone else who wanted to get into the act, they were off, hurrying toward Holly's pickup and their one-night honeymoon.

While they'd been speaking their vows, the front that had brought their earlier snowfall had passed, leaving behind clear skies, a pale winter moon and falling temperatures. Thanks to Jake's careful maintenance, the pickup's engine roared to life immediately. "C'mere," he growled, flipping on the heater, though he didn't activate the blower immediately. "I want you where I can feel you, Mrs. McKenzie."

It was what Holly wanted, too. Cold in her grandmother's wedding dress despite the warmth of her parka, she burrowed against him. She'd been wild about him from the first and now he was her husband.

Their ride home, over snow-dusted country roads, was swift, its progress barely impeded by numerous kisses. Before many minutes had elapsed, they were passing through Honeycomb's gate. Sheltered by its bare cottonwoods, the house waited, a single lamp burning in its living room window.

Fresh snow coated Holly's front steps. Though she was wearing cowboy boots, Jake wouldn't hear of letting her step in it. "You're my bride and I'm going to carry you over the threshold," he insisted.

She was shivering as he set her on her feet just inside the front door. "Darlin', you're cold!" he said worriedly. "Here . . . let me warm you."

"That sounds wonderful. I want you to do it—"

The rest of her words were muffled by a kiss. "What did you say?" he prodded.

"I want you to do it in our bed."

Tonight and every night from now on, they would share the same sleeping space, the same coverlet. Ardently but tenderly, Jake led her through her bedroom's open door. In anticipation of their lovemaking, Holly had dressed her four-poster with fresh, eyelet-trimmed sheets. Since they wouldn't wear nightclothes, her goose-down comforter topped several warm woolen blankets.

Tugging back the bed covers to make a place for her, Jake helped her out of her parka and cowboy boots first. Usually so graceful and capable, his big hands were awkward as they fumbled with the fragile, fabric-covered buttons of her dress.

"Here . . . let me help . . ."

Making a more adroit job of it, she finished taking off the dress and laid it over a chair. More with excitement than cold, she shivered again as she freed herself of its matching slip.

Jake wasn't sure of the cause. "We've got to get you under the blankets," he insisted.

"Not in my underwear."

Unhooking her bra and garter belt, and peeling down her filmy stockings, Holly allowed Jake to remove her panties. The brush of his fingers on her naked thighs ignited little fires in places the cold couldn't touch.

A moment later, she watched from the bed with the covers pulled up to her chin as he took off his things. How beautiful he is, how economical in motion . . . like some great, wild stallion, she thought, the hot interior place where she wanted him warming and opening a little more as her gaze followed the uneven seam of dark hair that pointed downward from his chest to his taut readiness. To think he wants me . . . that he let me put a halter on him. Before he could reach for them, she threw back the covers, offering herself.

The gesture was like a goad to Jake, who'd spent too many nights alone in his trailer and sleeping bag, wanting her. Getting in beside her, he pulled the blankets over them like a tent. They'd be joined at last, fused in ecstasy and body heat. First, though, he wanted to hear her helpless cries as he gave her a foretaste.

On Holly's mouth, his was like an avalanche—kissing, tasting, owning her moist depths tongue to tongue. But that was only the beginning of what he wanted. From there, his hot, damp nuzzling descended via her throat and creamy shoulders to the upturned mounds of her breasts.

They'd been starving for each other and now, it seemed, he planned to eat her up. Already her nipples stood like miniature volcanoes in their arousal. A little moan escaped her as he licked one tight, pink bud and then fastened wetly on it, to suck as if he'd draw the last ounce of sweetness from her body.

One of his callused thumbs teased her other nipple, flicking it back and forth with such seductive restraint that little stabs of longing pierced her body. Their deep, erotic connection with the place where she wanted him most was instantaneous.

Big with his craving for her, he insinuated himself against the blond-tufted mound that guarded her womanhood. Within its sanctuary, she'd gone liquid with expectation. "Jake...oh, Jake...I love you so much. Please...come into me," she begged, feverishly caressing the broad muscles of his back and buttocks.

It was what he'd longed to do from the moment they met. But he wouldn't go for it yet—not until he'd given her a preliminary ride to glory and assumed protection. "This way first, darlin'," he coaxed, his dark head disappearing beneath the blankets as he moved downward to insert his tongue in her velvety folds.

She shivered with delight as he positioned himself between her legs. Because he was *Jake,* the blue-eyed cowboy her heart hadn't been able to resist, the simple act of granting him that degree of familiarity increased her pleasure a hundredfold.

Yet it wasn't what surprised Holly most. Overwhelmed by the upward spiral of sensations he was evoking, she quickly realized the flutters of gratification and relief she'd achieved on rare occasions with Clint were about to be surpassed the way a candle flame is outstripped by a forest fire.

Meanwhile, for the first time in Jake's life, another person's fulfillment mattered more than his own. In his experience, a woman couldn't be hurried and, bent on satisfying Holly's most sensuous claims, he maintained an exquisitely slow, provocative pace. Paradoxically, a part of him regretted the seasoning he possessed to exercise in her service. How I wish I'd never known another woman, he thought, his nostrils filled with the unique perfume of her arousal. And that she'd never had another husband. How glorious it would be to approach this equinox for the first time together.

To Holly, the unknown women who'd figured in Jake's past no longer mattered a whit. From this night forward, he was hers, and that was all that counted. Tangling her fingers in his thick, dark hair, she let herself tumble beyond reason, the last vestige of self-control.

With Jake, she found, she didn't have to strain for completion. Or *try* to do anything. All he asked was that she lose herself completely in his affection. Carried up, up, up by the most intimate touch she'd ever known, she kept thinking she could go no higher. Yet against all logic she felt her delirium intensify.

Instinctively, she lifted her lower body from the bed as she reached the breaking point. Seconds later she was dissolving in ecstasy. Instead of stimulating her mildly, the way her previous experiences had, the paroxysm of shudders that claimed her threatened to sweep her away. Heat rushed to her face, a ruddy sensation, as if her body's thermostat had gone completely berserk. Only subliminally aware that she was moaning, she clung to the man she loved as he moved upward to cover her.

"Ride it to the end, darlin'," he urged. "Don't stop until you reach the last ember."

Safe in his love, she dared to accept. At last, she quieted. Her thighs ached pleasantly. Her face was buried against his neck. "Jake," she whispered at last, filled with love to bursting, "it's over. I want you inside me... where you belong."

They were just beginning to explore what the night could hold. Absorbed in pleasuring her, Jake had felt his arousal subside a little. Now, at her passionate request, it reintensified. He was a cannon primed for shot, a loving sword seeking the depths of its scabbard.

Too easily, the tangible result of his longing could make her a baby. Though the notion thrilled and delighted him, he didn't want it to happen yet. They needed time to be newlyweds first—enough time for him to set things straight. The last thing he wanted was to trap her with that kind of connection.

Having allowed the weed of his dissembling to flourish, he'd have to stifle his conscience a little longer or ruin his wedding night. Shifting his weight, he reached for a foil packet he'd placed in the top drawer of Holly's nightstand that afternoon. A heartbeat later, sheathed in protection and forgetfulness, he was riding high against her body for maximum contact as he led her back to paradise.

Chapter Nine

Their bodies sated and their passion for each other temporarily quenched, Holly and Jake were deep in slumber when car doors banged and tires crunched on the snow outside their window. It was fully morning. A bunch of people, from the sounds of things, were making an awful din. They seemed to be beating on pots and pans and shaking cowbells. Somebody was actually playing a harmonica!

Rubbing the sleep from her eyes, Holly surfaced for a look. *"Ohmygod!"* she exclaimed in panic. "Jake . . . wake up! We're about to have company!"

Struggling awake, her groggy-eyed husband confirmed that she wasn't imagining things. When they scrambled into jeans and sweaters without bothering to put on underwear and hurried barefoot to the front door, they were greeted by Lars, Emma, Lisa, Jane and a gaggle of laughing neighbors. Several of the men were carrying the wedding presents they'd left behind at the Tørnquist ranch the night before.

"What...what's this all about?" Holly stammered as her stepdaughter hugged her about the waist.

"Ain't you ever heard of a shivaree?" a wizened rancher who lived to the south of them responded with a grin. "It's a fine old Colorado tradition. We couldn't let you off the hook just because it happens to be Christmas!"

Their recollection of the good-natured hazing newlyweds sometimes received partially restored, Holly and Jake hastened to make their visitors welcome. While she set out trays of Christmas cookies and a kuchen she'd made the previous day for their breakfast, he put on the coffee and reconstituted several cans of frozen orange juice. Before long, everyone was gathered about her island counter, laughing, talking and munching.

Waking up a little more and exchanging a loving glance with Jake, Holly felt her satisfaction deepen. The three of us are going to be so happy together, she thought, looking forward to the moment when Jake would try on the sweater she'd made and Lisa would unwrap her Barbie-doll wardrobe.

It was only after their guests had gone and they were cleaning up the dirty dishes that a shadow fled across her contentment. Jake and Lisa had been drying while she washed and, for several moments, her new husband let the towel he'd been using dangle unused from his fingers. He seemed to be staring at the freshly washed coffee cups that were piling up in the dish drainer without really seeing them as a troubled expression drew his dark brows together.

It was early January. Having made love in their room after Lisa had gone to sleep for the night, Holly and Jake were dozing. At least, Holly was. Though he'd never been happier in his personal life, Jake was wide-awake, agonizing over the problem of telling her the truth about himself.

Except for the time he'd spent in Durango winning Dutch's case, he'd been absent from his legal firm for more than three months. Even stretching things, his sabbatical was up. His most lucrative client would be getting impatient. Dutch being Dutch, he'd want an answer—soon. If he didn't get one, he was liable to come looking for them. Yet Jake was afraid to level with Holly. What the hell was he going to do?

Peripherally aware he was wakeful and restless, Holly opened her eyes. She snuggled closer. "Anything wrong?" she asked.

He couldn't bring himself to seize the opportunity that beckoned. Instead, he settled for halfway measures. "I was thinking about Lisa and the other side of her birth family," he said. "I know you've told me that her mother's no angel. But what about her grandparents? They might be decent folks. It seems to me that she and they deserve a chance to know one another."

From a plateau of peace and tranquility, Holly's mood plummeted to one of irritation. "Whose side are you on, anyway?" she asked, giving him a speaking look.

"Yours. And Lisa's." He turned on his side to face her, the expression in his blue eyes disturbing. "I'm only trying to think of what's best for her."

As if *I* haven't done that since the day I married her father, Holly thought. "Maybe you didn't understand when I told you about my promise to Clint," she said, swallowing her impatience. "Lisa's mother neglected her. She was sexually promiscuous. And she did drugs. She's in prison now because she was convicted of selling them. On his deathbed, Clint begged me to keep Lisa away from her—and her parents."

Jake felt as if he were arguing a court case under false pretenses. In fact, he was, he supposed. "What did *they* do to deserve his mistrust?'' he asked, stifling his scruples and proceeding, anyway. "Are they drug dealers, too?"

Holly resented his interference in what she considered her personal business. Her mouth had taken on a set, rebellious look. "On the contrary," she conceded reluctantly, "they're wealthy, respected business people."

"Then I don't see—"

"According to Clint, they spoiled Lisa's mother rotten from the time she was a toddler. And you see how that profited them. Unfortunately, the potential for harm is a lot greater than the likelihood that they'd spoil Lisa, too. My greatest fear, as was Clint's, is that—when her mother's released from prison—they'd let her spend unsupervised time with Lisa...maybe even hand that innocent child over to her."

Jake was silent a moment. Knowing Dawn as he did, he could sympathize with Holly's predicament. Yet he'd embarked on making a point he hoped would soften her up for his eventual confession of his standing in the situation. Lawyerlike, he pursued his original line of questioning.

"As her guardian, you could put a stop to that, couldn't you?" he asked, knowing full well that Holly had no official status where the girl was concerned.

Holly grimaced. "Not if they got a judge to give them custody. As Lisa's stepmother and Clint's widow, I don't have the legal standing of blood relative. I'd probably lose if push came to shove. I don't think I mentioned it before, but they tried to take Lisa from Clint when she was six, based on the argument that he was an unfit parent. At the time, his great-aunt looked after her whenever he was absent on the rodeo circuit. The petition argued that, as a single, working father, he couldn't devote enough time to her care.

"We started dating shortly after that, and then he won a minor lottery prize. I quit teaching to marry him and their argument fell apart. A month or so later, the court ruled in his favor."

Having filed the suit himself, Jake knew everything about it there was to know. In representing the Hargretts, he'd only done what he was paid to do. They deserved representation as much as anyone. Nonetheless, he was abjectly grateful that Holly had forgotten the name of the law firm involved. Similarly, he blessed the fact that it was dark in the room and she couldn't read his discomfort.

"Did you ever think Clint married you so that he could keep Lisa?" he asked, covering his tracks.

Calming down a bit, Holly took the question at face value. "It may have crossed his mind that it would be an advantage," she admitted. "But he honestly loved me. Of that, I've never had any doubt."

Their discussion ended on that note and they were soon drifting off to sleep. Yet, the following day, Holly could sense that something was bothering Jake. Unknown to her, he was anguishing over the need to make a clean breast of things. Eventually he'd have to do it, of course. And when he did, he stood to lose her.

Meanwhile, it was past time for him to call Dutch. Mid-morning, though he still hadn't decided whether he'd tell the older man the truth or continue to prevaricate, he announced he was driving into town on a variety of errands. He got the shock of his life when he dialed Dutch's private number from the wind-buffeted pay phone at the local gas station.

"So you finally decided to call," his old friend and client hailed him sarcastically while he was still trying to decide what tack to take. "Damn thoughtful of you. Too bad you're a little late. I've traced the area where you've been calling from. It's only a matter of time before I locate my granddaughter myself. Thanks to Brent Fordyce's help, I have a court order demanding her stepmother produce her so a judge can rule on her custody."

For once, Jake was speechless.

"Handle this...or I will," Dutch threatened.

Too shaken even to think of informing his hard-nosed client about his marriage or the job he'd taken at Holly's ranch for the purpose of checking her out, Jake admitted he'd pinpointed Holly's exact whereabouts. "I'll take the matter up with her this afternoon," he promised, aware his words might be a death knell to everything he held precious.

"You'd damn well better," Dutch emphasized.

Holly was bundled to her ears, forking bales of hay into the bed of her pickup preparatory to servicing the herd, when he returned to Honeycomb.

"Come into the house.... I have to talk to you," he greeted her without preamble, a strong north wind all but snatching the words from his mouth.

As his wife and intimate partner, Holly knew at once that something was terribly wrong. Unerringly, her female instinct fastened on the gray areas of his past. A problem had arisen from one of them with the potential to drive them apart.

Leaning her pitchfork against the pickup without a word, she preceded him into the house and made a pot of coffee. Thank God Lisa's at school...that she doesn't have to hear this, whatever it is, she congratulated herself.

"Okay," she said, turning to Jake with steel in her eyes. "Let's have it. I don't think I can take the suspense."

He didn't know where to start. Beginning, middle or end, his story would be excruciatingly painful to her ears. "Tell me you love me first," he pleaded.

It was going to be really bad. "You know I do," she replied unequivocally.

Try though he would, Jake couldn't think of any further reason to delay speaking the truth. He might as well get it over with and take his chances. "The day I turned up at your gate," he confessed, "it wasn't by accident."

A chill feathered down Holly's spine. Who had sent him?

She had her answer a moment later. "The fact is, I'm not your average wandering cowboy," he admitted when she didn't speak. "I'm Dutch Hargrett's attorney and I agreed to help him find his granddaughter. From what little I knew of you, I thought there might be another side to the story, and when I saw you, I knew there was. I needed fresh air and a breather from the life I led, and I decided to stick around—document what kind of mother you were. I didn't consciously plan to fall in love with you."

For Holly, each word that fell from Jake's lips was like a bullet aimed straight at her heart. She seemed to freeze until it was as if she'd metamorphosed into a statue made of ice. To her shame, she'd fallen in love with Jake and married him, when all the time he'd been making a fool of her. His protestation that he'd fallen in love with her, too, fell on rocky ground.

"In other words, Dutch knows where we are," she said at last, desperately trying to cope. "Will you be serving his court papers on me yourself? Or will a sheriff's deputy come knocking at my door?"

Her helpless feeling of being a moth pinned to paper was painfully obvious to Jake. Whatever I try to do to help her straighten out this mess, she isn't going to forgive me, he thought. Not if I beg till my hundredth birthday.

"By tracing my calls to him from the pay phone in town, Dutch learned Lisa is in Bonino County," he admitted.

"But he doesn't have her specific address. Before he discovers it, we've got to put our heads together...."

Heartsick and gripped by the most debilitating anger she'd ever experienced, Holly was seized by a fit of shivering. She refused to let Jake touch her, let alone take her in his arms. By tricking her the way he had over something he knew was of paramount importance to her, he'd betrayed everything she'd held dear in him.

"Was there some reason you had to romance and marry me to carry out your research?" she asked, putting the width of the island counter between them. "No... don't answer that. Surely, as an attorney, you recognize a rhetorical question when you hear one. For the record, there isn't any 'our' or 'we' anymore. You may be my husband in the eyes of the law, but as far as I'm concerned we no longer have a relationship. I want you out of here in the time it takes to pack your stuff."

Though he argued and pleaded, protesting his love for her, Jake couldn't change her mind. She flatly declined to discuss the options he thought they still had in dealing with Dutch. She wanted a divorce. It was that simple, that heartrending.

"Make it an annulment," she stormed. "I ought to be eligible for one, don't you think, since you married me under false pretenses?"

Surrendering the field with an eye to doing battle another day when her shock and outrage had lessened seemed the better part of wisdom. With a clenched jaw and a host of self-directed recriminations, Jake retrieved his belongings from Holly's bedroom closet and put on his coat and gloves.

"Couldn't we at least talk about this a little more?" he asked, his blue eyes filled with the pain of her rejection as he lingered just inside the front door. "I *love* you, Holly.

And I always will. I'm on your side—and Lisa's—despite my
loyalty to Dutch...."

By now, Holly's anger was like a stone, taking up the
space in her chest usually allocated to her heart.

"Because of you and what you did, your client has a
crack at taking Lisa away from me and placing her under
Dawn's influence," she answered in a wintry voice. "Both
of our lives are up for grabs. With you on our side, we don't
need enemies."

She was dry eyed as she watched Jake tramp through the
snow by the corral and get into his truck. To be sure he left
and didn't double back, or so she told herself, she stayed at
the window until he'd driven through the gate. It was only
when she turned away and discovered she couldn't find a
comforting spot anywhere in her beloved ranch house that
the tears began to flow.

Once they started, there seemed to be no stopping them.
Great sobs racked her frame, causing her breath to come in
ragged gasps as she lay facedown on the bed where Jake had
prostrated her with so much pleasure and sheltered her in
what she'd believed was his undying love.

All the time she'd been falling for Jake and, later, telling
herself how lucky she was to be building a new life with him,
he'd been cheating on her in the most profound way imag-
inable. Why, oh, why couldn't he simply have come and
checked me out, if his job required that of him? she asked
herself. Being hunted down and handed to the Hargretts on
a silver platter would have been bad enough. Why did he
have to make me love him? And put me through the trav-
esty of a wedding ceremony?

Though her eyes were puffy and sore, she managed to pull
herself together—even to formulate some provisional plans
by the time Lisa got off the school bus and trudged up the
driveway. Unwilling to thrust the girl headfirst into the

controversy that was shaping up, but well aware she eventually would have to be told the reason for Jake's absence, Holly drew her down on the sofa by the fire and put a loving arm about her shoulders.

"Pumpkin, I have some bad news," she said, hastily adding at Lisa's look of alarm, "Take it easy. Comet's all right. This is about Jake. He's gone... this time for good. If we see him again, it'll be in a courtroom."

Lisa stared. "You mean... you guys are getting a divorce?" she croaked. "But... but... you just got married! Jake *loves* us. He wouldn't walk out on us. I *know* he wouldn't!"

With a show of calm and poise she didn't actually possess, Holly patted the girl's shoulder. Somehow, she had to make sure Lisa wasn't permanently affected by what had taken place. The fact that she was dying inside couldn't be allowed to take precedence.

"He didn't leave of his own accord," she admitted. "I threw him out. Early this afternoon, he told me the truth about why he came to Honeycomb. Instead of the cowboy he pretended to be, Jake is a lawyer hired by your Hargrett grandfather. There's every chance he'll help him file suit to gain your custody."

Expecting fear on Lisa's part, Holly was prepared to deal with it. She hadn't bargained for the volatile blend of anger and anxiety the girl displayed. Seemingly oblivious to the very real possibility that she and Holly might be separated, Lisa focused on Jake's departure and what she clearly felt was Holly's mishandling of a lovers' quarrel.

"Jake would never leave us without a good reason," she reiterated, her thrust-out jaw defying Holly to contradict her. "What did you do to make him mad at us?"

Though Holly tried a second time to explain who Jake really was and what his reason had been for showing up at

Honeycomb, it only seemed to make matters worse. As a result, she and Lisa were at odds for the remainder of the afternoon—a fact which added considerably to her emotional burden. Genuinely close and accustomed to being on an even keel with each other, they kissed and made up at dinnertime. But the problem between them was far from resolved and Holly knew it. She had only to meditate on the tenor of her stepdaughter's next remark to have an inkling of what lay ahead.

"I've been wondering..." Lisa said as they did the dishes. "Why would it be so bad for me to meet my grandparents? They might turn out to be like Mr. and Mrs. Tørnquist. And Jane loves them."

Without running down the Hargretts, who were—after all—Lisa's blood relatives, Holly did her best to make the girl see what was at stake. "If a judge gives them custody, they'll take you away from me," she said. "You'll go to live with them and I won't get to see you anymore. But that's not the worst thing that could happen. When your mother gets out of jail, they might turn you over to her."

Having heard about Dawn from Clint, Lisa made a face. "I don't want to be taken away from you, Holly," she said, putting down her dish towel and snuggling close. "I just wish Jake would come back—that things could be the way they were. It was almost like having a dad again."

In an effort to distract the girl from their troubles, Holly offered to take her into Larisson to see a movie she was enthusiastic about. When they got into the truck, however, the engine wouldn't start. Though Holly peered under the hood, she was no mechanic. She couldn't diagnose the problem. Returning to the house, she phoned Lars, who held his tongue when she volunteered the news that Jake was gone and promised to come over in the morning for a look.

Lisa sighed when she learned that they'd be staying home, after all. "Jake could have fixed the truck for us," she muttered rebelliously, driving yet another nail into Holly's heart.

In a somewhat acerbic tone, Holly reminded her that Jake was out of the picture for good. "We got along without him before," she said, "and we can do it again."

Usually so even tempered, Lisa answered with a sharp retort. "Jake's not a quitter any more than my dad was," she asserted. "He loves us, and he'll be back for us."

Each time Jake tried to phone her from Durango, Holly hung up on him. A week later, a fresh-faced sheriff's deputy from Larisson served her with the expected formal notice of a custody hearing. It was to be held in three weeks, in a Durango judge's chambers. Adding insult to injury, Jake had personally signed her copy of the petition in his capacity as Dutch Hargrett's attorney. "Holly, please contact me so we can work something out," he begged in a separate, handwritten note that arrived the same day via her regular postman.

With Jake's help, Dutch Hargrett was going to take Lisa away from her. She didn't have the financial resources to stop them. She couldn't keep herself from panicking. As she paced the floor after Lisa had gone to sleep, she remembered Clint had put keeping Lisa from the Hargretts first and preserving Honeycomb for her future second.

The situation called for desperate measures. Putting any notion of seeking an annulment or divorcing Jake on the back burner and blinding herself to the reality that what she was envisioning qualified as contempt of court, she came to a momentous decision. We'll run to Alaska if we have to, she thought. Dutch Hargrett and his daughter aren't going to shape Lisa's life if I have anything to do with it.

Recalling that the Tørnquists had wanted to expand their own spread by buying Honeycomb before Clint had come along and offered most of his lottery winnings for it, she phoned them while her stepdaughter was at school. When Emma told her to "C'mon over," she drove to their ranch and laid her troubles in front of them.

Characteristically, they asked what they could do to help.

"Buy Honeycomb from me," she answered, "for whatever you consider a fair price. The money will allow us to make a fresh start somewhere Jake can't find us."

Devastated by the news that the man who'd seemed so right for her had turned out to be allied with the enemy, the Tørnquists hesitantly advanced the theory that running away from problems never solved anything. When she was adamant about selling, however, they agreed to rent the ranch for six months and run her cattle with theirs. If she still wanted to sell at the end of that time, they'd buy the ranch and its herd from her.

Packing up their clothes, she announced to Lisa that they were going away for a little while. She'd taken a temporary job as a cook at one of the spreads north of Pagosa Springs to make some sorely needed cash. While they were gone, the Tørnquists would care for their cattle and horses.

It would mean changing school districts for the rest of the year, at least, and Lisa didn't want to go. She missed Jake and she would miss her friends. She didn't want to leave her filly and her life at Honeycomb. Yet this time the storm for which Holly had been bracing herself never materialized. In the final analysis, it appeared, Lisa loved and trusted her even when she was skeptical.

In Durango, the court date passed and Holly didn't appear. To forestall a warrant being issued for her arrest, Jake took it upon himself to get the case continued. Though it was an out-and-out lie, he told the judge the parties were negotiating.

For at least a week, Holly hadn't answered her telephone. Heartsick over the mess he'd made of things, Jake decided to drive down to Honeycomb and try to persuade her to give him another chance. Together, he believed, they could come to a solution that would benefit everyone.

To his dismay, he found the place deserted. Even the horses' stalls looked as if they hadn't been inhabited for several weeks. Pausing outside the barn with the collar of his sherpa-lined jacket turned up against the wind, he let the loneliness of the place wash over him. The life they'd begun together so lovingly was gone. So was everything that mattered to him.

Several minutes later, he was hightailing it to the Tørnquist ranch in search of information regarding Holly's and Lisa's whereabouts. To his frustration, though they still treated him like a friend, Emma and Lars refused to tell him anything.

Returning to Honeycomb, he let himself into the house with the key Holly had given him after they were engaged. The cedar chest containing her grandmother's wedding gown and other family treasures was still there, in the bedroom they'd shared. If he knew her, she'd be back for it before leaving the area.

It was Friday afternoon and he had a lonely weekend to waste. He decided to hang around. She and Lisa can't be too far away, he reasoned as he lay on the bed they'd shared, staring at the exposed ceiling beams. They're probably staying with friends. They'll be back, if only to get the rest of their things and say goodbye to a place they loved.

Unfortunately, it was a serious situation. By absconding with Lisa in defiance of a court order, Holly had flouted the law. She was risking arrest. I've got to find her, he thought. And fast . . . before this thing explodes in her face.

While Jake was holed up at Honeycomb, Dutch and his wife, Bernie, happened to lunch with friends at a favorite Durango watering hole. Among the locals at the next table was the judge who'd been assigned to hear Lisa's custody case. They belonged to the same country club. When Dutch stopped to chat after they'd finished their meal, he learned something interesting. The continuance had been Jake's suggestion.

Jake returned home on Sunday night to find an angry message on his answering machine. "Get your butt over here before I file a grievance with the bar association," Dutch's voice growled. "I want to talk to you about representing my best interests."

The session that followed in the older man's private office at the Flying D wasn't a pretty one. Reaming Jake out every which way to Sunday, Dutch vowed he'd have Holly arrested. "In case you didn't know it, Judge Markey is a friend of mine," he harrumphed. "He won't hesitate to issue a bench warrant on my behalf."

"You know where Holly is?" Jake asked, keeping a cool head. "I don't. She's gone from Honeycomb Ranch. And her neighbors won't tell me her whereabouts."

To his astonishment, Dutch did. A detective he'd dispatched to the valley on Saturday had stumbled across someone who, by chance, knew exactly where she was working.

Somehow, Jake had to save Holly from herself. He demanded to be told the details. "I swear to God I won't spirit her away or cooperate in anything illegal," he said when Dutch demurred. "Instead, I'll pick up Lisa for you. She can stay here, at the ranch, until the custody dispute's settled."

Irritably, though he betrayed a glimmer of satisfaction, Dutch agreed. When pressed, he revealed that a man who worked as a wrangler for one of Holly's neighbors had seen her in Pagosa Springs, buying large quantities of groceries. Partly out of curiosity and partly because he'd always admired her from a distance, the man had followed her back to the Lazy S, a huge commercial cattle spread owned and operated by a conglomerate. Incredibly, she was working there, as a cook in the bunkhouse mess.

The desperation to which he'd driven Holly made Jake wince. However, he'd promised Dutch he'd pick up Lisa and he'd keep his word. Ironically, though she'd hate him, it might keep the woman he loved from landing in a jail cell.

"I'll get right on it," he pledged.

Dutch gave him a caustic look. "Unless I miss my guess, you're sweet on Holly Yarborough," he observed. "If you weren't, you wouldn't have compromised your integrity to this extent."

That night, Holly dreamed of Jake and awoke with a heavy heart. She put a cheerful face on things as she saw Lisa off on Monday morning at the school bus stop. It would be her afternoon off and, keenly aware the girl wasn't happy in her new environment, she impulsively promised to pick her up at the end of the school day. Instead of Lisa sitting through the long bus ride home while Holly sat around and twiddled her thumbs, they'd go shopping in Pagosa Springs and eat hamburgers out as a special treat.

Somewhat lackadaisically, Lisa accepted. A short time later, Holly was hard at work, preparing a hot lunch plus a cold buffet supper the ranch hands would consume in her absence, when she was struck by a sudden sense that something was amiss. I hope to God Lisa hasn't been injured in a playground accident, she thought. That's about all I'd need to go crazy at this point.

The stress of hanging around until the Tørnquists were ready to buy the ranch was getting to her, she supposed. Pushing down her uneasiness, she cleaned the kitchen and returned to their private quarters to change clothes. At the appointed time, she was waiting in her pickup outside Lisa's school, watching a steady stream of youngsters in winter clothing come flooding through a gap in the chain-link fence.

Her uneasiness returned when no redheaded ten-year-old in a turquoise parka with a navy-and-white stocking cap pulled down over her ears came running to meet her. Is she making me wait because she's mad at me about something? Holly asked herself. Or did one of her teachers ask her to stay after for a moment?

Worried, she decided to find out. When a quick search of Lisa's classroom and the area near her locker didn't yield any sign of her, she was on the verge of panicking. Spotting the girl's teacher as the latter emerged from the principal's office, Holly hurried over to her. "Where's my daughter?" she said. "She didn't come out with the other children."

The woman blinked in confusion. "I thought you knew, Mrs. McKenzie," she said a bit defensively. "Lisa's father picked her up a few minutes early, for a dental appointment."

Incredibly, Jake had run them to ground again. Shivering like a hunted animal, she asked the woman to describe Lisa's male parent. The teacher's hesitant string of adjectives fit Jake to a T. He had Lisa. And he was taking her to the Hargretts.

"What was he driving?" Holly asked as calmly as she could. "A dusty red pickup?"

Lisa's teacher shook her head. "A silver-gray Mercedes. Is anything wrong?"

Without pausing to explain, Holly demanded to know what time they'd left. Seconds later, she was racing for her truck. Jake and Lisa were on their way to Durango with a ten-minute lead. If she broke every traffic law in the book, she might be able to catch them. Exactly what she planned to *do* if she succeeded didn't enter into her reckoning.

She'd gone just a short distance out of town when, suddenly, she was slamming on the brakes. A silver-gray Mercedes had caught her eye. It was parked near the gas pumps at a discount station on the lefthand side of the road. With the discovery came a break in traffic. She made a screaming U-turn.

Lisa was inside the car. "Get in... quick!" Holly ordered, reaching across the pickup's front seat to open the door on its passenger side.

Wide-eyed, Lisa did as she was told.

"Where's Jake?" Holly asked as they sped away.

"Inside the gas station."

Paying for gas, no doubt, Holly thought half-hysterically. In his haste to snatch Lisa, apparently, he forgot to check his gas gauge. Too bad he isn't wasting precious minutes in the rest room.

With a powerful car at his command, he'd be after them in a shot. On impulse, Holly turned into a run-down motel's parking lot and drove around to the side, where they'd be mostly hidden from view. Her evasive strategy didn't come a moment too soon. A heartbeat later, they were watching Jake's Mercedes speed past.

"He said he loves you—that he's trying to head off trouble for everyone," Lisa ventured.

Holly grimaced at what she considered a trumped-up excuse. "He sure found a funny way to do it," she answered bitterly. "He must have known I'd be out of my mind with worry when you turned up missing that way."

Hoping Jake would lose their scent, she decided they'd spend the night at the motel. Tomorrow, if the coast was clear, they could retrieve the few possessions they'd brought with them to the Lazy S. A quick stop at Honeycomb for family mementoes, and we'll be off, driving north through the mountains toward a fresh start in Alaska, she thought.

They'd be sitting ducks if they did either, she concluded the next morning, with a somewhat frayed night's sleep under her belt. The keepsakes at Honeycomb were the only things she cared about. Emma and Lars could send them to their new address.

In the interim, she had to select a route. With mountainous country on all sides, she didn't have many alternatives. Abruptly, the ghost of a smile played about her mouth. Our best bet is to drive *toward* Durango, and go on from there, she decided. Jake would never expect it.

Following a sleepless night filled with worry and calculation, Jake was trying to get inside her head. If I were Holly, and as blindly committed as she is to saving Lisa from Dawn, I'd do the least anticipated thing and head for Durango, he thought. He decided to drive that way and hope for the best.

Forty-five minutes later, Holly and Lisa were passing the Durango city limits. Because of seasonal activity on the nearby ski slopes, the town was crawling with tourists. They quickly found themselves in a traffic jam.

Jake's right behind us—I *know* he is, Holly thought, praying the riveting fear she felt wasn't communicating itself to Lisa. Desperate to keep moving amid cars that were bumper-to-bumper, she made a wrong turn and was forced to backtrack. Stopped at a red light, she looked in the rear-view mirror and spotted a silver-gray Mercedes.

There were a lot of red trucks in the world, including the one Jake owned. It was possible he hadn't seen them yet. What could she do? They were near the parking lot for the popular "smoke and cinders," coal-powered train that ran between Durango and Silverton. On impulse, she turned into the lot and paid an attendant to park. The train was about to depart and, without any coherent plan in mind, she caught hold of Lisa's hand. Together, they ran to the depot, where she bought two tickets, and hurried aboard, two fugitives in a mob of skiers.

Jake hadn't noticed Holly's red truck. Biding his time in the traffic, he happened to glance toward the train parking lot, which was more than three-quarters full. In his opinion, it would provide excellent cover for someone seeking to escape detection.

On impulse, he turned in, too. Several minutes passed before he located Holly's truck. To his chagrin, it was empty. They're on the train! he thought. Just then, the engine's whistle blew two short blasts. A column of smoke issued from its smokestack.

The train was about to pull out! Sprinting, he arrived at the track just seconds too late to jump aboard. He'd have to follow them in the car. His heart pumping like the engine's pistons, only harder, Jake forced himself to relax. Now that he knew where they were, he had plenty of time. He'd collect them at their destination.

Chapter Ten

Though they'd been expecting it, the train's sudden departure caused Holly and Lisa to lurch forward in their seats. From her position next to the window in the second-to-last car, Holly shuddered to see Jake standing there. Clearly he saw *her*. Having escaped him for the moment, they were every bit as trapped as if his lean, powerful fingers had just closed about her wrists like handcuffs.

So familiar, he seemed almost a stranger in his dark slacks and top-quality, sherpa-lined leather coat. His eyes were just the same—bluer than blue and intent on getting what he wanted. In the fleeting glimpse she got of him, with Lisa's reflection superimposed on it in the glass, she sensed frustration, anguish, tenacity. The man she'd loved, married and slept with so briefly was used to winning. If and when he succeeded in reuniting Dutch with his granddaughter, would he consider Holly's refusal to accept him anyway much of a loss?

With a Mercedes at his disposal, Jake would be waiting for them at the Silverton station. Meanwhile, her truck was parked in Durango. If somehow they managed to evade him in Silverton, should they try to hitch a ride back, and reclaim it? Or hop a bus for some destination farther along their route? If she chose the latter option, they'd be reduced to the clothes on their backs and what little money she carried in her purse.

She would do whatever it took to keep her promise to Clint. Chugging slowly through the town with its plume of smoke hanging overhead like grayish lace, the train gradually picked up speed as they passed a series of low-lying rural properties along the river. A few elk were grazing among the cattle. The highway—a straightforward ribbon of concrete—paralleled the tracks on the left. They could see the Mercedes beside them, keeping pace.

Their first glimpse of snowcapped peaks came twenty minutes to the north. Farther along, the tracks crossed a railroad bridge over the highway. Their path and Jake's diverged. While the highway took a high-altitude route, blasted from the shoulders of mountains, the train would chug up a narrow, winding river gorge, stopping for water once along the way. People lived near the water stop, and that meant a road. Would Jake be waiting for them there? Or would he continue onward, knowing he had them exactly where he wanted them?

Lisa chose that moment to slip a hand into hers. Though her lower lip wasn't quivering, there was an unhappy, confused look on her face. "Couldn't we trust Jake, Mommy?" she asked. "He loves us. He wouldn't try to make us do something that wasn't right."

I wish we could, Holly thought. Unfortunately, our entire relationship with him was built on a lie. Unable to think of an answer that wouldn't violate the girl's assumptions about the man she'd placed in Clint's stead as a father to her, she didn't say anything. Instead, she simply shook her head and hugged her stepdaughter close.

Beneath the train, which seemed to hang over the gorge, water tumbled over rocks. Snow glistened. Aspens shivered in their nakedness. As they continued to labor upward, Holly switched seats with Lisa and shut her eyes to the spectacular scenery on either side. Doing her best to let go of the tension that was eating her up, she lost herself in the squeak and groan of wheel flanges, the wail of the train's whistle, the clacking of its wheels over the rails. It was only a matter of time until Jake caught them. To all intents and purposes, she'd lost.

Hope revived as, some three hours later, they pulled into the station at Silverton. Retrieving their luggage and gear from the overhead racks, the skiers prepared to alight at the mountain-ringed resort. With so many people getting off at once, maybe Jake will lose us in the crowd, Holly thought.

While he was elbowing his way in search of them, they could be making their getaway on the other side of the railroad cars! Grasping Lisa's hand, she raced with her to the caboose, where souvenirs and hot chocolate had been sold during the trip. A quick look around informed her that the coast was clear. Hurriedly climbing down the steps, they crossed behind the caboose and took off, running as fast as they could.

When they reached Silverton's main street, which was overflowing with skiers and tourists on holiday, she hesitated, then turned left. Beyond the panoply of tourist-oriented shops, she spotted a small coin laundry. Perhaps there was a telephone.

Dashing inside with Lisa in tow, she found one, complete with phone book. Rapidly scanning the tattered yellow pages, she started to dial the number of a bus company that advertised ski tours. If they could nab a pair of extra seats ...

"Not so fast." Reaching past her, a strong hand severed her connection. With a sick feeling in the pit of her stomach, Holly turned to face the man she'd married and thought she knew. At close range, he was every bit as handsome as she remembered—and ten times more authoritative.

"You have no right to take Lisa...or power to arrest me," Holly said.

Jake's fingers tightened. "On the contrary. I'm an officer of the court. And you're a fugitive from justice."

The other women in the laundry were staring. "You want me to call the police, honey?" one of them said.

Slowly, Holly shook her head. Jake had won. It was that simple. If he was to be believed, she was in imminent danger of arrest. To retain any chance of seeing Lisa from time to time, let alone raising her the way she'd promised Clint she'd do, she'd have to cooperate. Ceasing all protest, she allowed him to lead them back to the station, where he was double-parked.

With an uncommunicative ten-year-old sandwiched in between them as if he were still driving her truck and living with them at Honeycomb Ranch, Holly and Jake exchanged few words on the return trip. Instead, they were lost in their private thoughts. Why, oh, why didn't he take Lisa away last fall? Why didn't he show his true colors, when he first came looking for us, Holly asked herself miserably. Why did he have to hang around and make me fall in love with him? Dissemble to the point of asking me to marry him?

On their way to the Hargretts' ranch, Jake pointed out a handsome log home and barn on what Holly would have termed a "dude ranchette" or weekend property. "That's

where I live," he said negligently, as if he doubted she or
Lisa would be interested. "I did a lot of the carpentry and
plumbing myself."

Maintaining her wall of silence, Holly didn't answer him.
But she was undeniably curious. Despite the money he'd
probably saved by taking on some of the work himself, the
house, its outbuildings and land had cost him a pretty
penny, she guessed. It had become increasingly clear to her
that, whatever his start as a "dirt-poor rancher's son" in
Idaho, he'd been quite successful. When she'd character-
ized him as a man used to winning, she hadn't been far from
the mark.

He didn't say anything more as his big silver car ate up the
miles that separated them from Dutch's place. All too soon,
he was lowering the power window on the driver's side to
punch in a numerical code on a keypad that was mounted
on a pole to the left of an electronic gate. The gate itself was
framed by tall stone pillars and a high electronic fence.

Somewhere, a computer processed his combination and
the gate swung open to reveal a winding driveway. At its
end, amid ponderosa pines, junipers and aspen, stood the
huge, somewhat ostentatious pseudo-Victorian mansion
that belonged to Lisa's grandparents. Having imagined it
many times, Holly had never expected to set eyes on it. Now
she was being brought there against her will, like a miscre-
ant to justice.

A uniformed butler opened the front door for them before they had a chance to press the bell. Immediately behind him were the Hargretts, who'd abandoned whatever
pursuits had been occupying them to greet their granddaughter in the mansion's marble foyer.

"Lisa, darling! You've come home to us!" sweet-faced
Bernie Hargrett exclaimed, rushing forward to throw her
arms about the shy youngster.

A smile of satisfaction and pleasure splitting his craggy countenance, Dutch joined them in a three-way hug. Obviously overwhelmed by so much affection from people who were, in essence, strangers to her, Lisa remained a passive participant. Watching them, Holly bit her lip. Unless she could convince a judge that she was a better parent than two blood relatives who obviously loved her and could give her everything she wanted, she realized, she had lost.

Keenly aware of her pain and the fact that he'd been its instrument, Jake lightly squeezed her shoulder, the words *It'll be all right* somehow inherent in the gesture. Flinching as if she'd been struck, Holly moved away from him. Don't even try to smooth over what you've done, she retorted silently. You can never make it up to me—*never* make it right.

Rebuffed, Jake hid his feelings behind a guarded expression.

For all her wealth and access to designer clothes and beauty treatments, Bernie Hargrett looked every inch the cozy grandmother. In a tense situation that rendered Dutch's business acumen useless, it was she who empathized with their discomfort and took charge of the situation.

"You two and Dutch will want to confer," she told Jake and Holly softly before her more combative husband could bark out the kind of orders that would raise hackles all around. Her bright eyes rested on Holly's face. "Would you mind if I took Lisa to the kitchen for some cookies and hot chocolate?" she added, asking permission just as if Holly weren't at a serious disadvantage and the Hargretts, at least for the moment, in the driver's seat.

From a reluctant accomplice, it turned out, Lisa had become Holly's staunchest defender. It was clear from the look on her face that she wouldn't go willingly without her stepmother's okay.

Holly gave it, feeling she had little choice. A moment later, Bernie was gently leading the girl away and Holly was staring after them. "Okay, Mrs. Yarborough, Jake…what do you say we step into my office and talk things over," Dutch suggested.

Closeted with Jake and Dutch in the latter's study, which overlooked forested, snow-clad grounds through a sweep of mullioned windows, Holly felt like a wild animal caught in a trap. She could chew off her paw and escape, a cripple, as forest creatures sometimes did. But not if that "paw" was Lisa. She'd fight Dutch to the finish for her stepdaughter if that was what it took.

Despite the real-estate-and-mining magnate's initially soft-spoken manner, fireworks quickly erupted in the session. Holding forth from behind his massive desk, Dutch spoke eloquently of grandparents' rights. He demanded to know why Holly had ignored a court summons. "A proper parent for a ten-year-old wouldn't flout the law that way," he lectured her.

His pious words provoked a storm of countercharges from her, most of them focused on Dawn Hargrett's drug addiction, criminal record and demonstrated unfitness as a parent. "You raised her," she accused, unintimidated by his glowering expression. "What kind of parent does that make *you,* I wonder."

About to blast her with a retort, Dutch was silenced by additional blistering words from her mouth. "Maybe I shouldn't have run out on the court summons," she admitted, disarming his most serious charge. "But what would you have done in my place? Obediently lay your head on the chopping block of so much money and influence?" Her emphasis was derogatory as she glanced at Jake. "You and your *lawyer* here used subterfuge to hunt me down and invade my privacy. Today, he kidnapped me on your behalf. I wonder what a judge will say to that!"

At least she didn't tell Dutch about our marriage, Jake thought. If his volatile client found out about *that* before he had a chance to settle things, he might find himself facing disbarment proceedings.

"Hold on," he said, finally going on the offensive. "I didn't invade your privacy, Holly. True, I came looking for you. And hung around so I could check you out as a parent. What was I supposed to do—serve you with court papers? Or send you a telegram? I didn't know your address. As for your supposed kidnapping..."

Her tone frozen but smoking, like dry ice, Holly faced him. "It took place. Lisa was a witness."

"It's Lisa we have to think about...Lisa we're here to discuss." The words were Dutch's. Biting down on an unlighted cigar in an obvious attempt to regain his cool, he fixed Holly with a baleful stare. "You're damn right I sent my attorney after you, young lady," he said. "If he 'kidnapped' you, as you put it, he did you a favor. A sheriff's deputy would have arrested you and thrown your butt in jail."

Offended by his manner toward her, Holly didn't speak. Jake chose to bide his time as he tried to call his keen negotiating instincts into play. Filling the vacuum, Dutch went on to speak of improved rehabilitation techniques and his hope that Dawn would emerge from her prison experience a new woman, finished with drugs for good and ready to take on adult responsibilities.

"Whatever her progress, my wife, Bernardine, and I are ready to do our best for the girl," he pontificated. "A child should be raised by blood relatives, if at all possible. Despite your history with her and her father, Mrs. Yarborough, you can't claim any kind of kinship with my granddaughter.''

His monologue fueled Holly's worst fears. Fond parents that they were, if the Hargretts were successful in winning Lisa's custody, they'd hand her over to Dawn just as soon as she was released. She was highly insulted that Dutch should dismiss the loving bond between her and Lisa so lightly just because they weren't genetically related. Didn't he realize some of the best families didn't rely on kinship for the bond that united them?

"Are you through spouting off?" she demanded bitterly when at last he fell silent. "If so, you should know a couple of things. I love Lisa every bit as much as if I gave birth to her. And I'll die before I willingly hand her over to you so Dawn can corrupt and abuse her. You may have physical possession of her at the moment, thanks to Jake and most of the money in Colorado. But I'll fight you to my last penny and my last breath, even if that leaves me bankrupt and homeless!''

Unused to being told off by anyone, let alone a slender, financially strapped young woman, Dutch had gone red in the face. He all but leapt out of his chair. Desperate to defuse the growing animosity between his premier client, a man he liked despite his abrasive qualities, and the woman he loved but clearly stood to lose, Jake stepped physically between the two of them and attempted to mediate.

"I agree with a lot of what Dutch has said," he confessed to Holly, braving what he knew would be her scorn and distaste. "Grandparents do have rights. And that's as it should be. In most cases, they're assets to their grandchildren. Despite Dawn's bad behavior, it wasn't right or fair that he and Bernie missed out on Lisa's early years. They should be part of her life today...."

Stung by his implied criticism of her failure to notify the Hargretts of Lisa's whereabouts, Holly muttered that she'd only been honoring Clint's deathbed request.

"Be that as it may," he answered, "I agree with you on some points, as well. In my opinion, allowing Dawn unsupervised visitation with Lisa would pose a serious risk. Though, of course, we all hope for the girl's sake that her mother can be rehabilitated, the statistics on recovering addicts are mixed. Only time will tell in her case."

Turning slightly, he addressed himself to Dutch, who'd plainly gone ballistic over the implied criticism of his daughter. "Until the verdict on her recovery is in, caution on Lisa's behalf is mandatory," he continued. "Meanwhile, I can vouch firsthand for the fact that Holly has been an excellent mother. She and Lisa are extremely fond of each other. It's my hope that some sort of compromise can be reached."

Holly's mutinous expression clearly stated, *Don't do me any favors*. In her opinion, any arrangement that gave even partial custody to the Hargretts was too dangerous even to think about.

Used to calling the shots and relying on Jake to back him up, Dutch was getting increasingly steamed. Aware of his feelings, Jake sensed a compromise might be more easily reached if they agreed to a brief cooling-off period.

"What would you say to taking a break in our discussion?" he asked, including Holly in the question. "In court, it's difficult to predict which way a judge will go, and some form of shared custody agreement, arrived at in advance of a hearing, might prove advantageous to both sides. We could give the matter some thought this afternoon . . . meet again after supper prepared to discuss practical measures."

Deferring to Dutch first, he got a qualified grunt of approval—for the cooling-off period, at least. He could only hope his remark about the unpredictability of judges would sink in once the mining-and-real-estate tycoon had time to reflect.

Holly gave the idea her blessing, though she was seething. She needed time to plan and Jake was offering her that. She might as well take advantage of it. Nonetheless, she was still furious with him. The moment they were out of Dutch's office, she let him have it with both barrels.

"If you know Dawn, and I gather that you do, you know shared custody would pose the same risk as handing Lisa over to the Hargretts completely," she raged. "She'd still be subject to Dawn's influence. To think I believed you actually cared about my stepdaughter! Like a fool, I saw you as a father figure for her, when all along you were only interested in doing Dutch's bidding and furthering your own cause with him! In my opinion, you're lower than low. How dare you sit in judgment on me after the intimate deception you pulled?"

Fortunately for them both, perhaps, a maid hesitantly intruded on their acrimonious tête-à-tête. "Mrs. Hargrett hopes everyone will eat together in the dining room this evening," she said. "Dinner will be served at 6:00 p.m. In the meantime, you and Lisa have been assigned a twin-bedded guest room on the second floor, Mrs. Yarborough. If you would care to go upstairs and rest, Lisa will join you in a little while."

Disposed to trust Bernie Hargrett somewhat, thanks to her friendly, noncombative manner on their arrival, and concerned that she and Lisa not be separated, Holly accepted. She turned to Jake. "Does this meet with your approval?" she demanded sarcastically.

Answering her with a look, he asked the maid for his jacket and went outside to pace the length of the Hargretts' snow-lined driveway and think about options. As he did so,

Holly was similarly pacing in her room, an ultrafeminine boudoir tastefully decorated in shades of pink. She'd managed to calm down somewhat by the time Lisa arrived with tales of a "kitchen bigger than our whole house at Honeycomb" and the palomino mare that was waiting for her in the Hargrett stables.

The expected seduction of Lisa by the Hargretts' largesse was already under way. Though it hurt like a stiletto in the solar plexis, Holly did her best not to take her feelings out on the girl. Instead, "I thought you liked Comet best of all horses," she reminded gently.

Following a moment's reflection, Lisa agreed that was indeed the case. But, "I like the idea of a palomino, too," she admitted sheepishly. "If we aren't going to see Comet anymore..."

"I *guarantee* we're going to see her again," Holly vowed, painfully aware of the tactical error she'd made in separating the girl from her familiar, much-beloved surroundings.

Lisa's questions about her grandparents and what would happen next in her life weren't quite as easy to handle. To Holly's surprise, despite the overwhelming stresses of the situation in which they found themselves—or perhaps because of them—both she and Lisa managed to nap.

Holly slept the longest. She awoke finally, in early evening, at the sound of a light tapping on her bedroom door. A glance told her Lisa's bed was empty.

"Jenny's helping Lisa with her bath and a change of clothes in another suite," the maid who'd led her upstairs earlier explained, naming a fellow domestic, when Holly answered the door. "Mrs. Hargrett said you're welcome to use the adjoining bath and any of the clothes that have been placed in the dressing room for your use. She thought you might like to freshen up before joining everyone else in the dining room."

It was already 7:15 p.m. Aware she'd have to hurry, Holly thanked the maid and shut the door. Having slept in her clothes the previous night, she immediately searched the dressing room closet. Dawn and I must be about the same size, she meditated ruefully as she pawed through a generous selection of sweaters, skirts, slacks and dinner dresses. To her relief, none of the garments appeared to have been used. Indeed, some of them still sported their expensive price tags.

In Holly's opinion, the outfits had been bought for Dawn by her doting parents and rejected because they were too conservative. Though she hated to borrow any of them, or to accept favors of any kind from the Hargretts, she was even more put off by the notion of bathing and wriggling back into her soiled clothing. Selecting a plain navy blue wool challis dress and matching leather pumps, she decided to capitulate.

Though the food was delicious, dinner with the Hargretts in their magnificent, crystal-chandelier-appointed dining room was awkward for Holly, to say the least. Jake's blue eyes blazing across the table into hers and Dutch glaring at her from its head didn't help. For her part, Lisa was silent, wide-eyed, clearly nervous over the hostility she could sense in the room but curious, too, about her newly acquired grandparents. Of the assembled diners, only Bernie seemed at ease as she graciously kept the conversation flowing around the shoals of everyone's displeasure and unhappiness.

Before he aired the ideas he'd formulated during his lonely walk, Jake decided, everyone needed a good night's rest. "I've been thinking, and it seems best to me that we resume our earlier discussion in the morning, rather than going at it again tonight," he suggested.

To his surprise, Dutch concurred. The look Holly gave him intimated that, if she never spoke to him or Dutch again, it would be too soon for her.

When at last the group around the Hargretts' dining table broke up, he took her aside in the hall to issue a demand and a warning. "If you want Lisa to sleep in the same room with you tonight, you'll have to promise you won't attempt to run off with her under cover of darkness," he said. "I guarantee the gloves will come off if you try anything of the sort."

Aware of the security fence that surrounded the Hargrett estate, Holly condescendingly gave her word. A short time later, Bernie kissed Lisa good-night and walked her to Holly's room, then joined Dutch in the sitting area of their private suite.

"Honey...I just learned something from Lisa I think you ought to hear," she said gently, resting one hand on his knee as she joined him on the sofa in front of their wide-screen television set.

Immediately, Dutch was all ears.

"Our granddaughter says Jake and Holly were married on Christmas Eve," she confided. "Did you know about that? If so, you never mentioned it."

Chapter Eleven

His already florid complexion flushing a dangerous beet color, Dutch blistered the sitting room walls with his choicest scatological terms. Pausing to remind Bernie that he wasn't angry with *her,* he stormed out of the room and ordered Evans, the family butler, to find Jake at once. "I want him in my office in five minutes!" he decreed. "No ifs, ands or buts!"

Guessing that his irascible client had somehow learned the full extent of his relationship with Holly, Jake braced himself for a firestorm as he complied with Dutch's summons.

He got exactly what he expected. From his position of authority behind the fortress of his desk, Dutch called Jake every name in the book. Accusing him of being a traitor to his obligations, he threatened a malpractice suit.

Irate as Dutch was, he managed to find a crumb of comfort in the situation. "Unless I'm misguided as sin," he gloated bitterly, "you're poison to Holly Yarborough now.

Maybe I should call her Holly McKenzie. If so, I doubt if she'll be using the name for long."

Jake didn't let his client see how much that likelihood hurt him. "I plan to change her mind about me," he answered with as much equanimity as possible. "Just as I plan to change yours. Somehow, we've got to deal with the fact that you and Bernie spoiled Dawn rotten... that you're still tempted to give her the benefit of the doubt when a child's welfare is at stake. I guarantee you Judge Markey will consider it."

About to escalate the hostilities a notch, Dutch struggled with his famous temper and appeared to win. Abruptly, he sagged a little in his chair. "You're right, son," he admitted in a tone that told Jake he was back in the older man's good graces. "We failed with Dawn, though the latest reports from her rehab counselor at the prison are hopeful. We're just selfish enough to want another chance with our granddaughter. What do you suggest?"

Breakfast was served buffet-style in a plush but tweedy dinette-and-family-room area that was dominated by a huge stone fireplace. Homesick for her own ranch as she filled her plate before the crackling blaze in a heavy sweater and never-worn pair of Dawn's jeans, Holly did her best to ignore Jake's unspoken hints that he wanted time alone with her.

Patently fast friends with Bernie, though she'd known her less than twenty-four hours, Lisa was chattering away about their planned trip that morning to the Hargrett stables and kennel. Reluctant to interrupt and be the odd woman out, Holly opened one of the glass sliders and took her plate of cheese strata, bacon and fruit out on the adjoining redwood deck. Placing it on the broad, comfortable railing, she rested her elbows beside it and stared pensively at a spectacular view of the nearby mountains as she tried to imagine what the future might hold.

She tensed when Jake joined her a moment later.

"We need to talk privately," he said, doing his best to ignore her obvious distaste for him. "Dutch knows about our marital status. Even so, we've managed to work out a compromise you might be willing to accept."

Holly's skepticism was evident in her deep sigh, the helpless shrug of her shoulders. Having spent the night under the same roof with him but in a separate bed, she was furious with herself for missing him—and with him for delivering her into Dutch's hands.

"Go ahead, tell me about it," she answered, making no attempt to be gracious. "You will, anyway."

So close that their shoulders all but brushed, Jake didn't make a move to touch her. "According to the terms we worked out, you and I would have custody of Lisa with visitation rights reserved to Bernie and Dutch Hargrett," he explained. "In return, they'd agree in writing not to allow Dawn time alone with her unless you gave your explicit permission."

Incredulous, Holly bit her lip. He hadn't finished yet.

"You may not be disposed to believe it," he continued. "I can hardly blame you. But the truth is, Dawn's counselor at the prison has given her a glowing report. Dutch showed me a copy of it. And it appears to be legitimate.

"Since entering a special program for drug offenders a year and a half ago, she's improved her behavior one hundred percent. She's reportedly recognized the factors that caused her to turn to drugs in the first place, and volunteered her understanding that staying away from them in the future will be an arduous, day-to-day struggle. She's enrolled in a parenting class for inmates at her request.

"As you might imagine, Dutch and Bernie are overjoyed at her progress. However they recognize that the odds against long-term recovery from an addiction like hers are formidable. And that they're more than a little prejudiced where she's concerned. They're prepared to let you decide when—or *if*—Dawn qualifies for time alone with Lisa. You'd have the arbitrary right to withhold your permission for as long as you see fit if you aren't thoroughly convinced of Dawn's rehabilitation and fitness as an alternative parent."

Jake paused, half-afraid to phrase the question that hovered on the tip of his tongue. "Mind telling me what you think about what we're suggesting?" he asked.

Stunned, Holly could scarcely believe Jake had wrung such far-reaching concessions from Dutch. Before quizzing him about how he'd managed it, she felt compelled to clear up her soaring confusion about one of the conditions he'd set forth.

"What do you mean, 'you and I' would have custody of Lisa under your plan?" she asked. "Aside from being Dutch's attorney, how do you come into it?"

By now they'd completely abandoned their breakfast plates. Courting danger, a small brown wren had alighted and darted forward to share their feast.

"Aside from being Dutch's attorney, I'm still your husband," he reminded her. "I expect to continue in that capacity. Despite what you may think of me, I love you deeply, Holly. And I love Lisa, just as if she were my own child. I want to salvage the life we promised to share on our wedding day. Fortunately for both of us, Dutch trusts me to see to it that any out-of-court agreement we reach is equitably carried out."

Something painful Holly couldn't articulate twisted in her gut. "And if we don't stay married?" she asked, unwilling to admit, even to herself, how much she still loved him. "Supposing I want a divorce. And the freedom to raise Lisa without your help."

Somehow, Jake had known she'd seize on that point. "You're right," he conceded with the greatest of reluctance. "Fair's fair. My presence or absence in your life shouldn't make a difference."

Her eyes narrowed even as, deep inside, she registered his unhappiness. "But it does ... doesn't it?" she asked.

Painfully, because he'd vowed not to lie to her again and he knew it was another way of losing her, he answered, "Yes."

Something closed in her face. "I'll have to think about it," she said.

Jake was silent a moment. "You realize this isn't totally about Lisa or her grandparents—that it's also about *us*," he said at last. "For what it's worth, I'm ashamed that I didn't tell you the truth about why I was there, at Honeycomb, right from the first. But in a way you might not understand or forgive, I don't regret it. If I *had* told you, I'd have been your adversary. We'd never have gotten to know each other."

At least she didn't turn him down flat. "As I said, I'll have to think about it," she reiterated, her voice bereft of any discernable emotion.

Jake did his best to smother his disappointment. "I'll leave you, then, so you can get on with it," he responded, picking up his plate and going back into the house.

Alone on the deck after he'd gone, Holly let the remains of her breakfast congeal on her plate. Outfitted with a pair of suede hiking boots that also belonged to Dawn, which she'd adjusted to fit by adding a second pair of socks, she decided to go for a walk.

As she strolled through the trees toward a little knoll, shivering despite the strong winter sunlight, she tried to sort through the muddled thoughts that were competing in her head. Despite her animosity toward him, which by now was ebbing, she still loved Jake with all her heart. The chance he'd offered to recapture the life they'd begun to share a shining possibility within her grasp, she grieved that he hadn't given her much of a choice.

If she refused to cooperate with the plan he'd conceived, she could lose Lisa and be forced to default on her promise to Clint. In her book, that was coercion. If she succumbed to it, she feared, her feeling of helplessness would always poison their relationship, just as her parents' relationship had been poisoned when her father had insisted that her mother accompany him to Alaska against her will.

Ultimately, though her mother had caved in to his demands, the divorce she'd attempted to stave off by doing so had come about, anyway. What on earth was she going to do?

To her surprise, the tracks of the Durango-Silverton Railroad were visible in the distance, through an opening in the trees. As she watched the morning train make its way up the valley preparatory to its long climb along the gorge, she reflected that she'd liked Alaska. Unlike her mother, she'd been sorry to leave it. In fact, the years she'd spent there as a child had been among the most colorful and exhilarating she could remember.

There was a lesson in the thought and, abruptly, Holly knew what it was. *Why fret over solving a problem you don't have?* she asked herself joyously. Your mom didn't want to go to Alaska. But you want to keep Lisa and stay married to Jake. What's stopping you? Pride? Your late mother's unhappy life? Your infernal stubbornness?

She still didn't like the fact that Jake hadn't been honest with her. Yet it was obvious to her by now that he'd suffered greatly for it. Secure in his love, she could afford to lay the matter to rest. The way things had worked out, she doubted he'd ever be so rash again!

Racing into the house with a little explosion of happiness and energy, she burst uninvited into Dutch Hargrett's study, where one of the maids had told her he and Jake were in conference. "I've decided to accept your proposal," she announced, looking from Lisa's grandfather to the man she loved.

While Dutch's craggy but affable face lit up, Jake's was a study in mixed emotions. He'd been thinking about the coercion angle, too. "Sure this is what you want?" he asked.

Holly's smile was positively luminous. "You *and* Lisa?" she exclaimed, putting her arms around him so lovingly that his anxious frown relaxed into a grin. "You'd better believe it. To my way of thinking, that's the bargain of the century!"

Bernie chose that moment to tap lightly on her husband's office door and enter. "Everything okay in here?" she asked.

"Couldn't be better." Dutch beamed.

Jake's response fell into the nonverbal category. With profound relief and humility over the second chance he'd been given, he was thoroughly kissing the woman he loved.

With his law practice situated in Durango while Holly and Lisa were still emotionally tied to the ranch Clint had bought for them, Jake and Holly still had a few things to settle. Fortunately, he didn't expect it to be all that difficult. Having learned a thing or two during his sabbatical and their time apart, he was planning some permanent changes in his life-style that would coincide with theirs.

Walking arm in arm with Holly down the driveway where he'd ambled in solitary reflection the day before, he told her how much he'd grown to love Larisson Valley and Honeycomb Ranch.

"The prospect of being a real rancher again, not just a tenderfoot with a weekend place, is more enticing to me than you can imagine," he confessed. "Viewed in the context of daily physical labor and fresh air, the gorgeous scenery I've come to take for granted and—most importantly of all— loving you and watching Lisa grow up, my life as a lawyer in Durango can't compete."

He wanted to live at Honeycomb with them! Though she was spilling over with happiness, Holly's forehead crumpled a little. "I don't want you to give up your legal career entirely," she objected, halting to gaze up at him.

Putting both arms about her waist, he reassured her as he tugged her close. "I've thought about it, and I want to remain a partner in Fordyce, Lane and McKenzie. I just plan to take fewer cases. If things work out the way I want them to, I might spend a few days a month here in Durango— maybe even a week or two now and then. But I can do a lot from Honeycomb via fax, telephone and computer. We'll need to expand the house a little, to make room for an office, my law books and a fax machine."

"Oh, Jake..." Holly's exclamation was part joy, part distress. She wanted to expand the house, too, so they could have a baby. But...

For once, Jake was oblivious to her mood. "I'm ready to go back today if you are," he told her.

A lump had formed in Holly's throat. "I hate to tell you," she said, "but the Tørnquists are renting the place."

His response was a grin. "Not to worry," he soothed. "We can easily straighten that out. If I know Lars and

Emma, they'll be so happy you and Lisa are happy that they'll tear up the lease forthwith.''

Back at the house, they told Bernie and Dutch about the decisions they'd made. Business clients as well as longtime friends of Jake's, they listened with qualified approval and a high degree of self-interest.

"What about us?" Dutch asked at once when finally he was able to get a word in edgewise. "Now that we've found her again, we want to spend some time with Lisa. We won't be able to do that if you take her back to Larisson Valley this afternoon."

In Jake's opinion, matriculating at a third school in as many months would be a disaster for the girl, particularly in view of all the confusion and upset she'd just endured. Despite the new horse and other treats that were in the offing for her in Durango, he guessed, she'd want to return to Honeycomb with them.

"I've been thinking about that, and I may have come up with a solution," he said. "First, we'll be back in Durango for the hearing next week to finalize our custody arrangement. But that isn't all. You have a motor home, don't you? As I recall, it's fairly luxurious. Why not come down to Honeycomb for Lisa's birthday? She'll be eleven in just three weeks. You could stay as long as you wanted."

Simultaneously, Bernie and Dutch turned to Holly. Their faces held an identical question.

Realizing he'd made free with an invitation before consulting her, Jake deferred to the pretty Scandinavian blonde who was nestled in the curve of his arm.

Assured of the Hargretts' discretion where Dawn was concerned, she sparkled up at him. "I think it's a great idea," she said. "It just occurred to me that, when school lets out in the spring, she could come to Durango for a month or so. Jake and I could use some time alone—a kind of second honeymoon.''

Lisa was elated when she learned the news. Hugging Holly first, she turned to Jake. A moment later she was nestled in his arms. "I guess this means you're my new dad-by-marriage...for keeps," she whispered.

For his part, Jake was thinking he couldn't have a daughter who was any dearer to him if she'd sprung from his own genes. If he and Holly had a baby girl someday, his daughters would be two peas in a pod when it came to his heart.

"You'd better believe it, sweetheart," he answered, his exceptionally gruff tone betraying the depth of his tenderness.

A phone call to Lars and Emma catching them up on the news easily persuaded them to vacate the lease Holly had signed. Though she, Jake and Lisa remained at the Hargrett estate for lunch, by early afternoon they were in the Mercedes, heading home to the ranch they loved.

As they approached the Tørnquist place, Jane was getting off the school bus. "Oh, *please!*" Lisa squealed. "Stop! We haven't seen each other for so long...."

Minutes later, they were having coffee and homemade doughnuts in Emma's cozy dinette while the two girls fairly danced around them with merriment. Following a barrage of congratulations and expressed happiness all around, it was decided Lisa would spend the night with Jane so the lovers' reunion wouldn't be interrupted.

"Just think...we'll be going to the same school again!" Jane rejoiced as she and Lisa disappeared down the hall to exchange confidences in her room.

As she and Jake continued home without their favorite ten-year-old, Holly recalled a loose end that hadn't been satisfactorily knotted. "There's just one small thing that still bothers me," she divulged.

Jake threw her a worried glance. "And that is?"

"I have a hard time understanding how you could pick up Lisa at school and make off with her without letting me know. Didn't you think I'd be sick with worry?"

Jake's tension evaporated. "Ah, but I didn't," he said. "As far as I knew, she was supposed to take the school bus home—a half hour's ride at the very least. She didn't tell me any different. I was phoning you from that gas station to tell you what had transpired when you caught up with us."

If it hadn't been for his generosity of spirit, he might have gotten away with Lisa's abduction. Instead of ending up together at the Flying D, where they'd been able to settle their differences, they might have met again in a courtroom. The outcome—and their subsequent lives—could have turned out vastly different.

"Thank heaven you're a principled softie at heart," Holly whispered, planting a warm little kiss on his neck. "Jake McKenzie, you easygoing lawyer, you...I love you so much."

Honeycomb Ranch welcomed them with its snow-covered meadows and distant mountains as if they'd never left. It was their home and would continue to be, at least until Lisa was grown. They could plant their roots deeply, without the fear of unspoken conflicts haunting them.

Their physical reunion started the moment they'd unlocked the front door. Unbuttoning Holly's parka, Jake slid it down her arms. "I want to touch you...worship you all over, darlin'," he said, running his hands down her body.

Dawn's heavy sweater and stiff jeans were in the way. "That goes for me, too," Holly answered, unwilling that the slightest barrier should separate them. "Don't you think we're a bit overdressed?"

The problem wouldn't be difficult to resolve. Pausing to adjust the furnace controls, which Holly had set at a chilly forty-five degrees prior to her departure, Jake lovingly drew her toward their bedroom.

Preoccupied though she was with what they were about to do, she sensed instantly that something was amiss. Seconds later, she realized that the down-filled comforter she used as a bed cover was rumpled, as if from the imprint of a body. She was positive she'd left it neat.

"Somebody's been in the house," she proclaimed worriedly.

Jake flung her a contrite look. "You're right," he said. "Somebody *has.*"

"You?" she asked in surprise.

He nodded. "I drove down over the weekend, hoping to put things right. And you weren't anywhere to be found. I stretched out on the bed to wait for you. Somehow..." He shrugged. "I don't know. Lying there, where we'd made love, made me feel closer to you, I guess."

All the affection he felt for her, all the longing, reverberated in the offhand confession.

"I'm here now," she whispered.

Seconds later, they were wriggling out of their clothes and climbing under the covers with nothing but their skin to separate them. How have I managed without this man? Holly thought in amazement as Jake's mouth blazed a sensuous trail to worship her breasts. He's in my pores, in my bloodstream. As the years go by, we'll be more and more a part of each other.

For once, she wouldn't let him bring her to culmination first. Instead, they'd reach the heights together. "I want you in me from the beginning," she asserted. "Just as deep as you can get."

Though it had been intensely satisfying between them since their wedding night, their reunion sparked their most earth-shattering coitus yet. Relief entered into it, but it wasn't the only cause. In a way they'd only grasped at earlier, they were truly married at last, journeying soul to journeying soul, locked in a profound embrace.

Thrusting high against her body, so that her face was buried against his chest hair and their sexual contact was exquisite, Jake primed the pump of their ascent. It wasn't long before Holly was fluttering at the brink and dissolving in a maelstrom of pleasure that seemed to implode and implode until she was at one with the universe.

Jake followed in seconds, unaware he was invoking her name like a blessing. At last they quieted. Heat radiated from their bodies, compounding itself wherever they touched.

With Honeycomb's animal population still in the Tørnquists' charge, there were no chickens to feed, no horses to curry. They could go to sleep if they wanted, though it was still daylight.

As Holly surrendered to the urge, Jake thought of Clint, the man whose untimely death had made all this possible for him. If your spirit's around somewhere, you can rest easy, old buddy, he whispered mutely to his predecessor. I love them both more than life and I'll take good care of them. I know how utterly damn lucky I am to have the love and trust of Holly and your daughter.

Someday soon, they'd make a little brother or sister for Lisa to love.

As if she'd sensed the desire he hadn't articulated to her yet, Holly sighed contentedly in her sleep. Her seeming

awareness of what he was thinking caused the corners of
Jake's mouth to lift. She was his alter ego, wasn't she? His
treasure and his beneficence. Why should he be surprised if,
on some subliminal level, she knew the loving thoughts that
drifted through his head.

* * * * * *

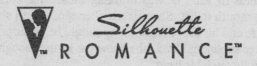

COMING NEXT MONTH

#1126 A FATHER'S VOW—Elizabeth August
Fabulous Fathers/Smytheshire, Massachusetts
When Lucas Carver's little boy picked the lovely Felicity Burrow as his mother, Lucas knew she was perfect. For Felicity touched his heart and mind in ways neither of them had dreamed possible.

#1127 THE BABY FACTOR—Carolyn Zane
Bundles of Joy
Elaine Lewis *would* keep custody of her baby—even if it meant a temporary marriage to her employee Brent Clark. But leaning on Brent's loving strength soon had this independent lady thinking of a ready-made family!

#1128 SHANE'S BRIDE—Karen Rose Smith
Hope Franklin left Shane Walker years ago to avoid tying him down with a child. But now Hope knew their son needed a father, and she owed Shane the truth....

#1129 THE MAVERICK TAKES A WIFE—
Charlotte Moore
Logan Spurwood had enough problems without falling for Marilee Haggerty. He had nothing to offer her; his past had made sure of that. But Logan couldn't stay away or stop dreaming of a happy future with Marilee.

#1130 THE MARRIAGE CHASE—Natalie Patrick
When heiress Felicia Grantham decided on a convenient marriage, no one could stop her—not even dashing Ethan Bradshaw. But Ethan's bold manner took her breath away, and soon Felicia was determined to follow her plan—with Ethan as the groom!

#1131 HIS SECRET SON—Betty Jane Sanders
Amy Sutherland traveled to the wilderness to find Matt Gray. He certainly wasn't the man she'd imagined as her nephew's father, but she hoped to persuade this rugged loner to accept the boy she loved.

New Year's Resolution: Don't fall in love!

Little Amy Walsh wanted a daddy. And she had picked out single dad Travis Keegan as the perfect match for her widowed mom, Veronica—two people who wanted no part of romance in the coming year. But that was *before* Amy's relentless matchmaking efforts....

Don't miss
NEW YEAR'S DADDY
by Lisa Jackson
(SE #1004, January)

It's a HOLIDAY ELOPEMENT—the season of loving gets an added boost with a wedding. Catch the holiday spirit and the bouquet! Only from Silhouette Special Edition!

HEARTBREAKERS

We've got more of the men you love to love in the Heartbreakers lineup this winter. Among them are Linda Howard's Zane Mackenzie, a member of her immensely popular Mackenzie family, and Jack Ramsey, an *Extra*-special hero.

In December—HIDE IN PLAIN SIGHT, by Sara Orwig: Detective Jake Delancy was used to dissecting the criminal mind, not analyzing his own troubled heart. But Rebecca Bolen and her two cuddly kids had become so much more than a routine assignment....

In January—TIME AND AGAIN, by Kathryn Jensen, *Intimate Moments Extra:* Jack Ramsey had broken the boundaries of time to seek Kate Fenwick's help. Only this woman could change the course of their destinies—and enable them both to love.

In February—MACKENZIE'S PLEASURE, by Linda Howard: Barrie Lovejoy needed a savior, and out of the darkness Zane Mackenzie emerged. He'd brought her to safety, loved her desperately, yet danger was never more than a heartbeat away— even as Barrie felt the stirrings of new life growing within her....

INTIMATE MOMENTS®
™ *Silhouette*®

HRTBRK4

HAPPY HOLIDAYS!

Silhouette Romance celebrates the holidays with six heartwarming stories of the greatest gift of all—love that lasts a lifetime!

#1120 *Father by Marriage*
by Suzanne Carey

#1121 *The Merry Matchmakers*
by Helen R. Myers

#1122 *It Must Have Been the Mistletoe*
by Moyra Tarling

#1123 *Jingle Bell Bride*
by Kate Thomas

#1124 *Cody's Christmas Wish*
by Sally Carleen

#1125 *The Cowboy and the Christmas Tree*
by DeAnna Talcott

COMING IN DECEMBER FROM

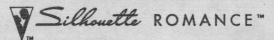

HE'S NOT JUST A MAN, HE'S ONE OF OUR

A FATHER'S VOW
Elizabeth August

From the moment single dad Lucas Carver saw Felicity Burrow, he knew she was special. His little boy knew it too—young Mark's first words were "Make Felicity my mom!" Felicity touched Lucas's heart in ways he'd never dreamed possible, and now Lucas was determined to win her!

Fall in love with our Fabulous Fathers!

Coming in January, only from

Silhouette
ROMANCE™

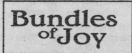
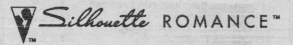